Beyond Forever

BEYOND FOREVER

We'll Meet Again

Diane Dowsing Robison

RESOURCE *Publications* · Eugene, Oregon

BEYOND FOREVER
We'll Meet Again

Resource Publications
An Imprint of Wipf and Stock Publishers
199 W. 8th Ave., Suite 3
Eugene, OR 97401

www.wipfandstock.com

PAPERBACK ISBN: 978-1-6667-8116-8
HARDCOVER ISBN: 978-1-6667-8117-5
EBOOK ISBN: 978-1-6667-8118-2

VERSION NUMBER 07/28/23

Contents

LOS ANGELES, CALIFORNIA
~~~ DECEMBER 1996

BARBADOS ⚜ 1837

Chapter 1 ❧ Souls Meet

He saw her for the first time standing on the cliffs overlooking the ocean when she was 16. Her long blonde hair was flowing in the wind, and her head cocked in a position as though she were listening to voices he could not hear. He was on horseback. He smiled as he came to a stop long before she was aware of his presence. He was 26 . . . blonde, tall, with an infectious charm, and a leader in command of his world.

It was a rough spring day on the island, and the waves were crashing with warning of an impending storm. He had no idea why he chose this way home to his plantation. All he knew was that from the time he spotted her tiny figure on the cliffs, he was compelled to move in that direction. He must have watched her for five minutes before she turned and smiled. She knew she was not alone, but when she finally turned around, her blue eyes widened, and a certain joy came bursting through her soul.

She knew instantly that this was the one human being who was going to change her existence for eternity.

As he moved closer, their eyes never left each other. Soon, they were close enough for the pleasantries of conversation. Though he had never seen her, she was well aware of him and his family's reputation on the island. They owned a large portion of it, and since his father had died several years ago, he had taken up the role of the master. He had also been instrumental in helping the island gain independence from the British. She liked everything she saw about this man sitting tall yet relaxed in the saddle before her. His dark brown eyes were like inviting pools, and his smile brightened the overcast day before her.

He was quickly aware that this was the young girl his family had spoken of. Sent to England to be educated, she had begged to come home to the island that held her spirit. For the past several years, she had constantly rebelled in school. Finally, her father capitulated and brought her back to Barbados. She arrived on the sailing ship only days before and had been the talk of the town as she disembarked. Instead of getting into the carriage waiting for her, she untied one of the horses, ripped off her skirt, flung herself up onto the saddleless horse, and raced home. As he watched her now, he sensed that this was a woman he would never get tired of knowing. What he knew without question was that they were communicating with a language much greater than he had ever experienced.

They were married less than a year later.

Chapter 2 ✑ Two Become One

T heir lovemaking was unending, and the continual discovery of one another was unmatched. The hunger each had for the other found a gentle evolution as they allowed themselves to be absorbed in each other's eyes . . . their hands and bodies only reflecting the dance that their souls guided. She bore him five children in six years: three sons and two daughters. When she asked him if he was getting tired of seeing her pregnant, he smiled as he placed his hand on the roundness of her belly, "There is nothing you could do that would make me tired of being with you —the least of all, bearing the creation of our love." She laughed her infectious laugh and rolled into his arms, where safety and calmness prevailed in a world that was rough and unrelenting.

They could never seem to get enough of each other, and the layers of their joy built as their life did. Their minds were a perfect match, and they faced all decisions together, respectful of each other's opinions, and they were rarely wrong as they became leaders of their new community. Their spirit and souls only complimented each other on every level. She taught him to become a risk taker . . . that life if anything, was built on challenges. He learned to laugh at things he once thought were too serious to find humor in, but his laughter was always based on the knowledge that he was blessed to have her by his side. He elevated her to the highest level of womanhood. He worshipped and cherished her and told her that there wasn't anything she couldn't accomplish. From him, she learned that she possessed an elegance and bearing that would have laid untapped had he not surrounded her with an invisible aura in which she could grow and blossom.

Chapter 3 ✑ Island Rebellion

T en years after they were married, rebellion came to the island. The British were unhappy to have lost this island rich in sugar and spices. A war broke out that ripped the heart out of the island and left the land again burnt and untamed. He was mortally wounded close to the end of victory for the islanders—and she got to him as he lay dying. She begged him not to leave her. He only had time to tell her that he would be with her forever . . . that when she needed him, she would feel his presence.

Chapter 4 ✦ Alone Here

She raised her family and helped pull the island together. She did it for him, but a fine layer of life had been removed from her existence. Oh, she found laughter in many things, but nothing made her heart sing . . . nothing made her want to reach out and embrace life in the way she once had. Only when she could feel him watching her did she remember what she was born for.

She was born for him, and he was gone. However, he was present in her children and the land she so loved around her. But the sea was the only thing that made her feel calm and content. When she looked at the sea, she knew he was somehow feeling the same things she was feeling. Although many tried to court her, she never married again despite the encouragement from her five children, adults of whom she was now so proud. She became the leader he was supposed to be—and never a year went by that she didn't think that, surely, he could have done it better. She lived thirty long years after his death, and when her time was near, she embraced it, knowing—on sheer instinct—that he would be there for her.

He was.

The Other Side . . .

He was as she knew he would be . . . strong and full of life. She had shed the age of her body and was once again everything she was when they were together. Their bodies seem no different as they first stood opposite one another— but their gaze told the whole story. They lost themselves in one another's eyes and, once again, talked without speaking. She, as before, could not look at him enough— could not drink in enough for her soul to be satisfied.

He smiled with a smile of indescribable contentment as he pulled her close to him, "Welcome home, my darling." He knew he was complete once again. As she placed herself within his arms, she experienced a feeling of belonging even greater than she had known on Earth.

And yet, their journey had just begun. But first, their souls needed to be calm.

THE RMS LUSITANIA
MAY 1st 1915

Chapter 5 ✍ Boarding

N ew York. It was raining as the passengers hurried to board the pride of the Cunard line, the "Queen of the Seas," as she was affectionately known.

He had boarded earlier but came to the rail overlooking the gangplank to smoke a cigarette and watch for a woman he had never met.

He saw her through the rain—dashing madly, holding up her ankle-length skirt in the distance as the rain soaked her short, bobbed hair. Quite the daring fashion since most women wouldn't think of cutting their locks of femininity. She was traveling with an older woman, of whom she seemed very protective as she slowed her pace, reached back, and grabbed the woman's arm to guide her up the plank.

He watched in amusement. She was the toast of Broadway. He had seen her in several plays and had always been amazed that this young 22-year-old woman could play such a range of parts. Having attended West Point, he grabbed every chance he could to head for New York City—a city he felt very comfortable in. Now, at 28, he thought back to the first time he had seen her on stage. She had to have been only 16, and yet her stage presence made everyone else seem dim in comparison. "Too bad she's so young," he had commented to a fellow cadet that night after walking out into the crisp air on 44th Street. "Yeah, but she won't be young forever," his friend had said with a wink. As he thought of that now, he smiled, threw his cigarette overboard, turned towards his cabin, and whispered, "How true."

The whistle blew at half past eleven, right on schedule, as the *Lusitania* was guided away from the dock. On board were 1,959 people—159 of them Americans and 123 children. The orchestra played "Tipperary," followed by the United States National Anthem. Soon, the captain's voice came over the loudspeaker, "All passengers, please assemble in the grand ballroom in one hour."

She made her way through the crowded ballroom, guiding her beloved "Grandmama." Appreciative of the kindness of strangers as they made room for her, she was growing weary of the frequent stops by people congratulating her on her stage accomplishments. She mentioned to her grandmother that she was still upset that their long-awaited trip had been publicized in the New York paper the day before. Her grandmother's only reply was to remind her that she had a great gift—and that a part of that gift was how she touched others.

"Compliments are a small price to pay. It's good for people to be able to reach out in appreciation," she said as pride for her only grandchild once again welled up inside her, making her walk seem somewhat easier.

"That's what applause is for, Grandmama," she replied as they reached a seat at the far end of the room. "Here, we're part of the real world and should be afforded a little privacy." Shortly after insisting that her grandmother sit as she stood behind her, the captain stepped up to the microphone.

"Ladies and Gentlemen, unfortunately, I was asked to remind you once again that as a state of war exists between Britain and her allies and Germany and her allies, all ships sailing under the flag of Great Britain are at risk of being attacked. Therefore, all passengers travel at their own risk. However, as you know, most of the world considers this grand ship, the fastest ship on the Atlantic run, to be an American ship. And, as America is not at war, we should all be safe. Besides, the *Lusitania* can attain a speed of 27 knots and can therefore escape from any attack . . . no one would dare attack the Queen of the Seas!"

The applause continued until the captain made a motion for it to stop. "I look forward to seeing you all at dinner—and please, enjoy this memorable voyage!"

She quickly maneuvered her grandmother back to their cabin, where she insisted she lie down. "You fret over me too much, my little darling," her grandmother said as she stretched out on one of the narrow beds.

"No, Grandmama, it is you who have taken care of me all my life . . . and this trip will be perfect for you. You haven't seen England since you were seven. Now you're going to show me all the things you've always told me about . . . and I'm going to be sure you're rested for our grand adventure! It's selfishness, pure and simple."

"You haven't got a selfish bone in your body, my child," her grandmother replied as she started to doze off. "But you are as stubborn as your Irish grandfather; God rest his soul."

Chapter 6 ❧ He Finds Her

W atching her grandmother rest, she walked over to the porthole and lit a cigarette. Definitely, something her grandmother could never approve of (along with the rest of the provincial world) for "proper young ladies." Of course, she knew she was not a proper young lady. She was an artist who was forced to grow up too fast. But she was from strong working-class stock, of which she was fiercely proud. This trip was important to her, but in a way she couldn't define. For now, she could only stand in awe of the magnificent ocean rolling past her. What a creation! And she was part of it . . . something she had always longed for from the confines of New York Island.

By May 4th, the *Lusitania* had reached the halfway mark, and the seas had calmed—something the passengers appreciated. Many started walking the decks in the brisk, cold Atlantic wind. As late afternoon approached, she insisted that her grandmother take her nap while she went out on deck to watch the sunset.

Leaning against the rail, with her back to the wind, she repeatedly tried to light a cigarette when a clear voice near her said, "That's not the way you do it." Startled, she turned to see a strong man with chiseled good looks smiling at her. A sense of calm came over her that she had never experienced. And, for a moment, although she tried, there was nothing she could say.

No painting he had seen in any of the world's great museums had ever compared to her as she stood there with the setting sun backlighting her body. Although he could barely see her features because of the sun's rays, a luminescence was present that had nothing to do with natural light.

He stepped next to her, took her cigarette, placing it easily between his lips, faced the wind, cupped his hand, and lit a match. His eyes never left her. The cigarette took hold right away. As he handed it to her, he said, "The trick is facing the wind—all good sailors know that. My father always said, 'Face the wind whenever you've got a problem.'" A moment passed as she took the cigarette. Her hands were shaking—from the cold—she told herself.

"Your father was a sailor?"

"Oh yes, the best . . . an Admiral . . . so, he was not thrilled when his son went to West Point."

"You don't like the sea?" she asked inquisitively.

"I love it . . . but I love flying more," he responded as he took her untouched cigarette back and threw it out to sea. "You don't need this," he smiled.

"Are you going to tell me that it's not proper for me to smoke?" she asked as she raised an eyebrow.

"No, not at all . . . I'm just saying that you don't need this." With that, he wrapped her arm around his and guided her slowly but gently across the deck.

They walked around the deck with no particular destination. Awareness of each other was their only focus. Talking came without effort, and neither felt a need to hide anything.

She learned of his love of football, which he had played at West Point, and opera, which he couldn't get enough. A man of opposite extremes, she thought. No . . . a man who transcends the typical palette of human colors, she corrected herself. And the color was what she kept seeing as she walked with him. An aura glowed around him—one she felt included her own presence.

She surprised him with her knowledge of the newly emerging world of "moving pictures."

"You're fascinated by them, aren't you," he replied.

"Good appraisal," she responded, encouraged by the fact that he was one of the few who realized that she was capable of more than the usual banal discussion of those her age. "This new technology will change how we perceive the world—and maybe each other. I would give anything be in California—to be part of the thrust behind what will set this old world on fire."

"Behind the scenes—no glory for an actress in that," he chided her.

"Ahh, glory comes in many forms," she laughed lightly. "The lasting kind usually comes from behind the scenes."

Brains and talent—he was continually surprised by her. This is a total woman, he reflected. A woman I think I want to spend a long time getting to know. He found himself smiling at the thought, which, up until this point in his life, had been foreign to him.

When they reached her cabin, it was time to wake her grandmother for dinner. They parted, each with a twinkle in their eyes, and promised to meet tomorrow.

The following two days moved all too swiftly for both of them. Whenever it was appropriate, he would join her and her grandmother. But the late night was theirs. They would walk the ship and share every detail of their lives and their thoughts. Soon, it was no surprise to either that the images in the deepest recesses of one were the shared image of the other.

On the night of May 6th, they walked the entire ship at least four times, knowing that tomorrow both would be busy packing for their arrival in England. As they approached her cabin, they stopped. He turned her towards him, the moon becoming a backlight for their bodies. He leaned down, and their lips brushed lightly. Transfixed, the kiss ignited a heat within them as they stood looking into each other's eyes—their faces less than an inch apart.

"From this day forward, you shall always be a part of me," he whispered, not moving.

"I think . . . you have always been a part of me," she replied.

Slowly, he kissed her once again. As their lips parted, he brought his hands up to cup her face. For some reason, he needed to study her every feature, as though to burn it into his soul. Her hands touched his, and then she turned slightly to kiss the palm of his hand.

"Sleep well, my love," she whispered. He knew he had to let her go but sensed that it was probably the most difficult thing he would ever do. She turned and started to open the cabin door. She turned back only to smile and form the words, "God keep you well."

Chapter 7 ❧ The Perilous Morning

Before dawn on May 7th, the *Lusitania* was within thirty miles of England when the British Admiralty warned Captain Turner that U-boats were in action along the Irish coast. Off of Cape Clear, the liner ran into thick fog. The captain reduced his speed to 18 knots. It would now be possible to cross the last few miles of the Irish Sea in obscurity and reach Liverpool safely.

At 8:00 AM, the captain ordered a reduction in speed to 15 knots, and at 10:00 AM, the ship passed the remote Fastnet Rock in the Atlantic Ocean at a distance of only twenty miles from the coast. Half an hour later, a radio message warned the *Lusitania* about enemy subs in the southern area of the Irish Sea. Captain Turner changed course slightly and brought her closer to the Irish coast. At 11:30 AM, the Irish coast was visible from the deck. At 1:45 PM, the grand "Queen of the Seas" returned to her normal course. A periscope was spotted only minutes later, and an alert was raised, but it was believed that the lookout was mistaken.

A U-20 watched the approaching ship and realized that it was the *Lusitania*. At 2:12 PM, one torpedo was fired. An explosion occurred, which shook the ship violently.

He raced out of his cabin to find her. Panic was erupting everywhere. The captain hoped to save the ship by grounding it on the beach. The speed was 18 knots, but the intercom was not working, so his orders were not heard.

Somewhere on deck, he spotted her trying to find safety for her grandmother in the confusion around them. He raced to her and put a firm arm around her grandmother. "I've got to get you to the lifeboats," he shouted above the voices around them.

As they approached the side of the boat, which was beginning to list, officers placed passengers in the first lifeboats lowered into the sea. He forced the two of them into the lifeboat. She tried to refuse because she did not want to go without him—and her grandmother kept repeating that "those with a full life left to live" should take her place. He ignored their pleadings and got them settled in the boat. She quickly realized that she now had no choice and must attend to the emergency at hand. Helping to settle in her grandmother and several others, she looked up at him as the boat lowered. Their eyes held—and immediately, they were silently communicating with each other.

As the officers were lowering the lifeboats, the order from Captain Turner to "*cease lowering*" was given. One officer ignored this command and continued.

From the rail—as he watched the most precious thing in his life descending below him—he felt a second large explosion coming from the area of the boilers. It knocked him and everyone around him down. He pulled himself up—just in time to watch her lifeboat shatter as it hit the props beneath the water. All aboard immediately disappeared.

There was no reality for him from that point on.

The ship continued to take on water, the turbines broke down, and the bow started sinking beneath the water. The communication system wasn't working—and lowered lifeboats on both sides were thrown into the water. The *Lusitania* was beginning to roll on her side.

Suddenly, he heard a young child's cry and turned to see a beautiful redheaded girl at his side. Her presence was the only thing that brought him back to a conscious state. Quickly, his body responded as he picked her up.

"What's your name, sweetheart?"

"Muriel Lee Smith," she said through gasps and tears. "I'm eight years old." Her well-trained reply brought a flash of a smile to his mouth.

"Well, Muriel Lee Smith, we're going to find a way for you to be safe," as he started making his way to the starboard stern where he could see other lifeboats safely landing in the water. Immediately, he knew this child was the most important thing in the universe. Somehow, she represented the only part of life that was dear to him.

"You're going to be all right, Muriel, I promise you," he found himself saying. And, the whole time, all he could see were the eyes of the woman he knew he could never really live without.

At the stern, he reached the side of Madame de Page, a woman who had somehow kept calm and had gathered an assortment of 35 children around her. He helped Madame secure two of the last lifeboats and safely placed the children in them, including Muriel. It was all entirely surreal for both of them. Keeping the children calm while getting them into the rafts and pushing adults away to protect the children seemed to take hours. It was now 2:30 PM, only eighteen minutes since the first explosion. A lifetime had passed before him.

Their job done, he convinced Madame de Page to climb down the ladder and jump into the sea. He followed immediately behind her. A sense of survival took over—perhaps the children had rekindled it in him—and they swam as fast as they could away from the sinking ship. Finally, when he stopped and looked back, he saw the stern high in the air and the four props visible. He saw a human clinging to the stern. By this time, the bow would have been resting on the seabed. For a few minutes, the scene remained the same. Then, with a deafening sound and clouds of spray, the *Lusitania* disappeared beneath the water. Bodies were floating around him—the sea littered with children and adults, dead and alive. In the distance, he could see the first ships approaching for the rescue.

Of the 1,959 passengers, 1,198 had perished. He saw no reason why he should have been one of the "lucky" ones.

Chapter 8 ❧ Alone Here . . . The Other Side

When he finally reported to his unit based in Washington, DC, his only focus was to kill an enemy who would knowingly destroy a ship full of civilians. His wait was agonizing, but he sealed himself from life and trained well in anticipation that the US would go to war. Almost two years later, in April 1917, America declared war on Germany. A few weeks prior, German subs had destroyed three American cargo ships. With the thoughts of the *Lusitania* still firmly implanted in the country's mind, these latest attacks were finally the straw that broke the camel's back.

The Other Side . . .

Once again, she found herself without him. She recognized the calm that she possessed and understood completely why she was there. Occasionally, when he calls to her, she sees him clearly as he moves on Earth's plane. She can feel his pain, his frustration, and his love. She sends him her love, knowing he is too blinded to feel it. She knows only too well that he still has work that has to be done on Earth. And she has *so much* that she still needs to understand here. But, since there's no time element for her here, she can rejoice in the knowledge that she'll see him quickly. For her, "now" is actually . . . today, and yesterday, and tomorrow.

By allowing her to go over what's already transpired in her growth, her guides gave her the opportunity to see what can lay ahead for her. It's like looking at a master blueprint of a house built in stages. As she turns the large pages, she can see what she's accomplished so far and what remains to be built upon.

It becomes so clear to her. So many choices—and so many paths. No wrong directions, just so many of them leading to the same place. She's fascinated by her transformation. As she observes where she's been—and makes decisions about where she wants to develop next—she's amazed at how his presence plays a part in the result of so many choices. Their paths will cross on earth if each follows the destiny they know is right for their own growth.

Will he be with me, she ponders, no matter where I am? She slowly recognizes that life everlasting is not something one has to grasp in one gulp. And perhaps she's learning that no real fear exists when holding on to the very thing that gives one the most life.

Is this the ultimate choice of which there should be no need to choose?

Chapter 9 ⮑ Battle of War Planes ... The Other Side

England, France & Germany. July 21st 1917:

B y January 1917, Germany's Manfred von Richthofen had secured his 16th air victory. He received the coveted "Blue Max"
for becoming the top German Ace . . . earning him the title of "The
Red Baron." He was 25 years old, and before the war was over, he
would claim 80 air victories—flying, as all the young heroes of the
sky did, in a wooden and fabric aircraft.

The air was still in July, projecting a strange sense of peace
over Germany. The morning was warm, and the German coun-
tryside looked like an inviting quilt to an American captain flying with his 2nd Lieutenant. The captain had come to love this
part of the world—the enemy's land seemed not at all strange
to him. It would have invited him to happier thoughts had his
focus not driven him towards the solitary road of destruction.
One German flyer, the Red Baron, represented everything evil
in this war—one man he could blame for erasing all he valued
in life. And this was the morning he would find that evil. As the
German and American planes spotted each other, a ritual dance
began with music being played by machine guns.

The sky was littered with smoke and planes, but the captain spotted von Richthofen and headed directly for him. As von
Richthofen pulled away at the last moment, the captain shot and

hit the Red Baron. Seconds later, a German aircraft from behind riddled the captain's plane—exploding it before it hit the ground. Manfred von Richthofen landed safely but suffered such terrible wounds that would affect his flying for the rest of his days. Seven short months later, the task that the young American captain had started found completion. A British officer brought the Red Baron down permanently.

⌒

The Other Side . . .

As a spirit emerges from its earthbound body, it finds a light that baths it—giving it life and form in a dimension not experienced on earth. That light also acts as a beacon leading the spirit to safety—to souls he's bonded with many times.

He found her as he walked through the light. She was there as he expected her to be. As his plane exploded, he knew no fear—her voice had been with him continuously until he saw her.

But the subconscious memories that remain in the soul can overshadow the direction of our growth. Driven by his lack of "completion" on earth, he refuses to accept that his soul needs rest. Fighting against a higher knowledge—he's compelled to return. His only hope is that she will follow.

Reluctantly, she does.

Confused and unsure, she's learned what's needed to advance her from the bonds of a deeply consuming relationship; the dangerous sword of love and anger will brew in her as she tries to find closure in the world that awaits.

NEW YORK
DECEMBER 1941

Chapter 10 ✑ Alexa

Rushing down crowded 5th Avenue, she pulls the coat closer around her—God, she loves this city! It is the only place she feels any sort of permanence. At 23, she's traveled most of the country and many parts of the world. She loves the Mediterranean—any town or village dotting the azure blue sea. But still, there is nothing like New York. Her family—very wealthy and very proper by nature—have a growing concern that their youngest daughter has no desire to even consider matrimony. Every time her mother delicately approaches the subject, all she can say in return is (with a wave of her hand and a wink of an eye), "Not this time around . . . too much to do!"

She's now a journalist of quality with a flair for finding something in a story that no one else thinks worthy. War is on the horizon, and she knows if she plays her cards right, she will be one of the first women in Europe to cover the action. Not bad for an old maid! What she does hate are these stupid suits, with their short skirts rising even higher in the bitter wind. Oh well, at least it was better than those ridiculous fashions of long skirts and petticoats her mother had to wear when she was growing up. I wonder why any woman would have put up with them, she thinks as she crosses 5th Avenue heading towards Rockefeller Center.

Her publisher, James Osborn, had the newspaper's editorial offices in this magnificent edifice of modern architecture. The New York Daily can't compare with the New York Times—but was a great starting place for her when she came begging for a job several years back. Just out of finishing school (having been "presented to society" at her debut the weekend before), she felt she'd done justice to her parents' wishes. Now, it was time to do something meaningful. But who would hire an 18-year-old writer with no real-world experience? Against his better judgment, her father called in a favor with his old schoolmate, the editor at The New York Daily. He knew that Fred would at least take a meeting with her.

"Just give her a few minutes and send her on her way," her father had said.

"No problem, Frank, but I know you better than that. Do you think she has any potential?"

"Unfortunately . . . yes. In more ways than you can possibly imagine," was his quiet reply.

It had been a hot, humid day in the city, and the meeting that was to last a few minutes stretched into an hour. Fred started her the next day as "copygirl." She loved running around, doing the bidding of every writer in the office. She also loved putting in her two cents on everything from headlines to photo layouts. Her natural enthusiasm was contagious, so her interfering was not only tolerated but encouraged. She wanted to learn everything she could, and everybody obliged her. She listened well. It soon became apparent to Fred that she could handle things that most newspapermen took years to master. Her first writing assignments were pretty lightweight—weddings, society stuff, and human-interest stories.

About two years after she started writing for the Daily, a fire broke out in a tenement on the lower east side. They were short staff that day, and she convinced the editor, Fred, that she should cover it. He relented, and she dashed out, promising to stay clear of danger. Fred had great faith in his newest protégée. However, he also knew her well enough to have strong doubts that her common sense would keep her out of harm's way.

Fred McDonald was 22 years her senior and now one of the best newspapermen in the business. He knew the streets of New York, and he knew human nature. He'd never seen writing like hers in such a young person—straight-forward, honest beyond her years, and incredibly insightful. He was a devout Catholic, married to his high school love, and now the father of strapping, teenage twin boys. He'd witnessed the best and the worst life in his chosen profession. When she came along, he thought that life had few surprises left.

Cynicism was a by-product of most good newspapermen, at least those who elevated themselves above hack-writer status. Fred stood five-foot, eleven-inches with a rock-solid build and unruly black curly hair that showed a hint of red in the sunlight. A strong man with a strong presence, he was quietly awed by her uncommon talent and slightly unnerved by her soft presence whenever she was in the room. As energetic as she was, there was something almost ethereal about her. His desire to protect her was constantly at war with the knowledge that she sorely needed experience on the streets to fully develop her potential.

She left for the fire with the full belief that she would stand on the sidelines and write what she saw. But what she saw disturbed her. Children—way too many girls in their young teens—were flooding out of the building that was now becoming a raging fire. This didn't make sense. Surely the Triangle Fire years ago had put a stop to children working as slave labor in garment factories. As she tried approaching some of the children, a man stepped forward to stop her. He was a short, ugly man, looking years older than his face indicated. When she told him that she was a reporter and asked why so many children were in the same building, he responded that they were part of an orphanage. When she said that it was odd that so many were girls about the same age, he snarled at her and told her he had no more time for her—whisking away the ten or so girls he had around him.

The streets were becoming thick with smoke, and the building was collapsing rapidly. The firemen worked as fast as they could to contain the fire to that one building. The other tenants, who were now safely a block away from the fire and debris, were too confused to answer her questions.

The Red Cross arrived and was caring for everyone as best they could. When she finally got a chance to talk to them, she inquired about the young girls . . . but nobody had seen any of them. She did find out that two elderly people were the only fatalities, which was amazing for an inferno that had so quickly engulfed the old structure. She spent the next hour looking for the man and the children around the nearby buildings. The only thing she found was the wrath of several firemen who sternly warned her to get as far away as possible. Only when one finally shouted at her, asking the name of her paper, did she decide that she had done as much as she could.

When she returned to the office, there was so much soot and ash on her that washing her face only made it worse. After going over her notes with Fred, she convinced him to let her follow through on her hunches in the morning.

"Okay, I'll make a few calls to city hall and see what I can dig up, 'off the record,' from a friend. At least we can get some history on the building."

"That's great, Fred; I appreciate it. I just felt so helpless once I got there. I knew there were some missing pieces but had no idea what I was looking for."

"That's called experience, kid. It was a pretty big assignment for you—not your average high-tea at the Plaza. Were you scared?"

"Scared . . . no. At least not until I saw my face in the mirror! 'Not in control' was more like it – and that's not a feeling I enjoy."

"Well, according to a call I got a few minutes ago, that's not how you acted."

"Huh?"

"Next time a fire chief tells you to get away from a collapsing building, I think you'd better take his advice . . . or at least not let him see you where you're not supposed to be."

"Ahh, now *that's* good advice—thanks, boss." She winked at him as she picked up her coat to leave.

"And the next time I find you put this paper in danger, you'll have a lot more to worry about than bricks falling on your head."

"Hmmm, that's even better advice. I'll remember that," she responded as she headed out of his office.

It took her two weeks of hard investigating, but the story she turned into Fred was more than anyone expected. She exposed a child trafficking ring that used "imported" foreign labor to work in sweat factories "hidden" in tenements. Parents from Eastern European countries would scrape together enough money to get their children to America—thinking they were being put in schools, for which they also sent monthly money. Instead, these young girls would be put to work in factories and, when old enough, put on the streets for prostitution.

Comparisons uncomfortably raced through her mind when she was working on the story. When she was the age of those girls, she was tucked in at night with a kiss—and home was a place where she had the privilege of being loved. The idea that children were being abused and going to bed frightened each night, when they should be protected from the world, drew a flash of anger through her soul.

That had been a pretty heady experience for someone who had just turned 21—but as far as she was concerned, a hell of a lot more productive than deciding what dress to wear for the latest social event.

The next two years give her plenty of experience. Eventually, she was allowed to cover everything from political fraud to murders. Somehow, through it all, she never lost that sense of optimism that should have been beaten out of her. Even on the brink of war, the world felt good to her. With Hitler on the rise, that sounded crazy even to her. Maybe what felt good to her was her place in it. There was something deeper she was sensing—something beyond the immediate injustice of right and wrong. And she was moving towards something, but she had no idea what. She couldn't shake the underlying feeling that she had to outrun time.

Now New York seems sweeter than ever. It's a cold winter day. Christmas and all its glory is around the corner. She's just left her parents after their Sunday brunch at a small, elegant hotel that bordered Central Park South. They had attended the late service at St. Patrick's cathedral and, for reasons that couldn't be defined, she found comfort in that large, massive structure.

Maybe, it was because it was the only time all week that she slowed down enough to hear or feel some contact beyond her own personal thoughts.

For a Sunday, the streets are unusually busy. She smiles to herself as she ponders this. Everybody must have been drawn into the city by the dazzling display of lights, getting an early start on the season's shopping. She looks at the buildings that give New York its personality. They've never felt like they're closing her in; the canyons of buildings only represented activity to her—so many people living so many diverse lives.

Passing the ice-skating rink in Rockefeller Plaza, she picks up her pace. She is in a hurry to get to the office. She has several hours of writing ahead if she is to get a jump-start on tomorrow's deadline. The crowds are particularly heavy here, and she needs to push through to get to the enormous gold and copper doors that serve as the entrance and stand as the centerpiece of the complex. Once inside, she slows her pace long enough to say 'hi' to the guard. The smell of the massive lobby always catches her off-guard. In her mind, it is a mixture of wax, stone, and sheer wealth. As she heads for the familiar bank of elevators, she enjoys the sound of her heels on the marble floor. The clicking of her shoes sounds like music notes that echo slightly against the high ceiling and again back to her. She's leaving her mark, vibrations that will be caught in this building forever, she muses.

When the elevator lets her off on her floor, she pulls out her keys to open the door to the reception area and is surprised to find it unlocked. Across the unending floor of desks, phones, and typewriters, the editor's office stands, with only glass walls separating it from the usually chaotic floor. She can see Fred with his back to her. He seems transfixed on something out the window. The radio is on in his office, so she shouts to be heard as she approaches his door.

"What are you doing here? Even the pathetically overworked has a right to be with his family on Sunday!"

As he turns around, his eyes are glazed. "I just tried calling you. The rest of the staff should be here within the hour."

She's never heard his voice like this, and in a fraction of a second, she feels like time's been suspended. She hears an urgency in the voice on the radio but is too focused on Fred to listen to the announcer's words. "For God's sake, what's wrong?"

"The Japanese just bombed Pearl Harbor."

Chapter 11 ᧽ December 7th

T he rest of the day becomes a blur. All she remembers was that when she finally left that night, the city had come to an eerie standstill. The staff had spent hours in the office trying to come to grips with reality and plan an attack for covering a war they knew would be fought on every front. The next day, the President made it a reality in an address to Congress.

Over the next week, her arguments with Fred become their opening morning gambit.

"You're too damn young, and you're too damn inexperienced!"

"Oh, good—let's send someone older. Maybe, one of the remaining males on this staff you haven't already assigned to Europe—with a family that can't do without him! This is just bull. You know I can find stories."

"No! I'm not sending you to a war zone!"

"Okay. Then at least, let me go to Hawaii. I can't think of any safer place now that they've demolished our Navy. Surely there's a military transport you can get me on. Let me cover the human interest side. I can go to the hospitals and . . . "

"Hell, they could bomb California for all we know!"

"Yeah—well, New York isn't that far away from the Axis' reach either! Or do you think Hitler isn't going to join the bombing party!?! Come on – no one's safe. What a coup for you! A reporter gets the human-interest stories from a woman's perspective when others only report who's alive and who's dead! Don't you think that every mother in America . . . "

And so it goes. Finally, Fred gives up. Attrition has always been her specialty. He pulls some strings and gets her on a military cargo transport heading for Hawaii three days later. First, she signs a piece of paper that's far beyond her experience to grasp. Soon, she'll discover that this single-page contract with the government will govern her life as a journalist while suspending every instinct she's ever developed.

The reality of what lies ahead—what she'll see and experience—is also too far out of her understanding. Maybe that's for the best.

Chapter 12 ∽ Across the Pacific

Oahu, Hawaii:

Fred's first chance to talk with her is two weeks after she arrives at Pearl Harbor. Using her femininity—a great advantage she found in a war zone—she's been given access to a secure military phone early one morning. It is still the height of the workday for Fred in New York. But then, his workday is at least 16 hours now that they publish both a morning and late-afternoon edition.

When he picks up the phone, her voice cuts through him. "Hi! How's the weather in the land of civilized people?" Her voice bounces through the phone line. It takes him a second to regain his strength.

"I don't know—I'm not out in it much. They've brought a cot and shackles for me in the back room, just in case I think of going home at night. And you? How's the weather in the land of leis and hula skirts?"

"Kind of unique . . . Christmas and hot weather. No real lights—everything's blacked out at night."

"Here too. They're not taking any chances anywhere. Last thing anyone wants is a few bombs to compete with the lights of Christmas. You'll be happy to know that I hired—in your honor—two-woman reporters today."

"Ha! You're just running out of men! Do them a favor, Fred; let them earn their stripes."

"You've obviously forgotten who you're talking to."

"You know, you really should have gotten an education – it's 'to whom you are talking.'"

"Ah, you can take the lady out of the upper crust, but you can't take the upper crust out of the lady."

"Well, I'm not feeling much like a lady right now – at least I can wear pants all day without my mother telling me they're 'inappropriate!'"

"Oh, by the way—*please* write your parents. If you have any regard for this tired, aging editor, you'll get them off my back."

"Come on; you know that you love their phone calls. It makes your downtrodden Irish soul feel you're mixing with high society."

"I'm going to let that one pass, kid. Look, your last two stories really hit home. It's a good balance with what we're getting from Jim in England."

"Ah, yes. The woman's touch."

"Well, I wouldn't say that the pictures you sent from the hospital and airfields held back on the gore—but you got the point across. I'm just sorry I couldn't print most of them. That freelance shooter does good stuff – let him know I said so. The guys' stories are great—I almost ran down to enlist."

"You're too old! Although, I bet you'd be a mean son-of-a-bitch facing the enemy! Look, Fred, I want to investigate something—and no one's saying much about it. It has to do with what went on just before Japan bombed us."

"Don't tell me it's something to do with the military? If it is, you're stepping out of your parameters, kid. You know the rules—and that piece of paper you signed makes it very clear. Everything, and I mean *everything*, has to be cleared by the military."

"Fred, I'm reading the daily papers you sent me. Picture this. I'm sitting at an outdoor restaurant on the beach—or what's left of it. I'm reading your article about how 'light' our damages were, as quoted by Colonel Knox when he met with reporters in New York. I put the paper down and look up. I'm looking out at *devastation*. I count five United States battleships—the Arizona, the Oklahoma, the California, the Nevada, and the West Virginia . . . resting on the bottom! And that's just the beginning."

"I don't care what you're looking at! Americans—*and* the Japs—need to be fooled into believing that we can win this goddamn war!"

"For the *love of Mary*—the Japanese papers have every hit in detail!!! Who the hell are we protecting, for God's sake?! What happened to that piece of paper called The Constitution?!"

Neither speaks a word for several long seconds.

"Kid, there's an Office of Censorship now . . . and if we want to stay in business, we comply. That's one more reality of war. Do you *really* think that any reporter in this country likes this?! It makes my skin crawl. But I *will* keep this newspaper afloat."

"Come on, boss, let's take a reality check. The last time I looked, we were a newspaper looking for stories! I can't report what they *won't* let us tell, but I can snoop around. All I'm saying is that there's a couple of things that don't make sense to a lot of people here."

"Like what?"

"Like why the aircraft carriers were not in port the morning we were bombed. Or, better yet, why they were out to sea without escorts?"

"Shit! That is NOT what you're supposed to be covering! We're all doing our part . . . "

She cuts him off with an anger that's not part of her nature. "And censorship for the American public is a part of that!?!"

Fred takes a deep breath, realizing he's arguing against logic. His only concern now is to get her home safely. "Look, we're walking a very thin line here. I don't want this paper's credentials pulled and frankly, I don't relish seeing your head lopped off by the military. You're just too goddamn stupid to know when you're stepping in quicksand. STOP snooping around and do what the hell I tell you to do!"

"*But* . . . "

He's angry. As a hardened newspaperman, he doesn't know if it's because he realizes she's potentially getting in over her head or because the press is in an unethical position. Why in the hell did I let such a greenhorn get in this position, he thinks. "Damn it—enough! End of discussion!!! Are you reading me?"

She quickly realizes what a short leash she's on and that he can pull her back to New York whenever he wants. "Okay . . . I think I get the picture . . . boss."

"And, stop calling in your stories. I don't care how secure you think those lines are; use the wire service."

"I hate typewriters; they don't go fast enough . . . and I can't spell."

"Well, *that's* a new revelation."

"Sarcasm is definitely your trademark. I'm glad to see that it's still alive and well. Face it, boss, you're just jealous that I'm here, and you're stuck *there* running the paper."

With that sentence, she hits a cord that even he had to admit was too close to the surface. "Enough, kid. Just do your job—and keep out of the military's way. And use the damn service!"

"Yeah, I love you too. Bye."

As soon as they hung up, Fred—disturbed at a greater level than his blood pressure needs to be—decides to call his source in the Pentagon. If she's right, I have to know, he reflects. The kiss-ass military in the Pentagon won't give him an answer, but what they don't say will be just as revealing. He almost smiled as he picked up the phone.

Chapter 13 ∾ Heading to Destiny

T alking to Fred earlier today proved overwhelmingly unpro-
ductive—but she had to try. We live to fight another day;
God-willing, she thinks as she jumps into the jeep the Navy so
graciously loaned her. She heads to the officer's club, another
friendly invitation from an obliging captain. Being a woman is
definitely advantageous at times; she muses as she starts up the
jeep. She loves the freedom of the jeep—traveling across the sand
and dirt in the open air. She needs a little R&R.

The moon is high tonight. How odd she thinks the beauty of
the moon is considered a danger. Its light baths the island—and
only a few short weeks ago, it would have been perceived as ro-
mantic. Now it represents a beacon for the enemy.

What she didn't tell Fred is that she's thrown up every day
since arriving. The carnage across the island, the edifices of half-
burnt ships still clogging the harbor, and the men in the hospitals
are testing her moment by moment. Hell in paradise; images she
will never forget. The price of growing up, she reflects. As a reporter recently said to her, "After this . . . you can never go home
again." For her, home represents safety, a strange insulation from
the world. That, however, is the last thing she craves.

Chapter 14 ∽ Jack

H e looked older than his 24 years—but then, everybody did. There are now no children left. Football games, bonfire rallies, and walking hand-in-hand in the show are a distant memory . . . far away from the reality of war, broken bodies, and blood. Soon, eighteen-year-old men will be shipped all over the world, and back home, young women will be filling the factories. Men who reach their mid-twenties will be lucky to be alive. Taking responsibility for saving a civilization—foot by foot across several continents—ages you fast. And the freedom of *not* knowing what you've seen no longer exists.

Yet only the invincible nature of youth carries the military forward. Even from the perspective of his young age, he hopes that no other generation will ever have to experience the carnage man inflicts upon man. A foolish thought, he recognized as he made his way to the officer's club. His love of history has taught him that man will always want to possess *more*—the nature of the beast.

Seeing the writing on the wall, he'd left college and enlisted in the RAF two years ago. Oddly enough, these last few months in North Africa has given him a glimmer of hope for the world's salvation. He found that the few experienced in leadership from previous battles were a rare but brilliant breed. On their shoulders, he sincerely hopes God is riding. Pulling up to the officer's club that tropical star-filled night, he ponders; the men who've trained him are walking with destiny—hopefully, one day, they'll become a living anachronism. Winning a war for the survival of a world free of tyranny, will place them in a position of obsolesce. But, not him, he once again assures himself. He'll fight this damn bloody war and be on his way. He has the world to conquer and knows that something important is awaiting him.

Born American in the windy city of Chicago, he jumped at a chance to go to Oxford for college. His father's alma mater in his mother's homeland had never been far from his mind growing up. His summer visits to England gave him a sense of belonging to both worlds. As he became a young man, his most substantial identity was within himself, unrelated to any particular geography. He'd always felt comfortable in any class or culture, thus becoming a man of the world long before entering college. His mother teased him that he was an "old soul." And, while he never took a lot of stock in it, he certainly appreciated his ability to understand human nature on a grander scale than most of his college friends.

By 1939, he felt that two years at Oxford was more than enough. Hitler was now gobbling up as much of the world as the pacifists would let him. His decision came while visiting his grandmother in London. It only took one air raid for him to know that he could never stand by while the world was crumbling.

His only experience with flying had been with his father, who let him take the stick in an old biplane when he was a kid. That was enough to know that his destiny in this war would be in the skies. The RAF trained him, made him an officer, and sent him to fly aerial reconnaissance in North Africa, tracking Germany's invading armies as they quietly moved further through the desert.

But with the bombing of Pearl Harbor, he became acutely aware that his allegiance must be to the United States. There was never any question in his mind, though his doubts about FDR convinced him that America would probably enter the war too late to make a difference. Frankly, he didn't care what plane he flew or uniform he wore when he shot down the enemy. All that counted was that the bastard died.

But he believes in America's rugged individualism and ability to rise when all things seem hopeless. And, at this point, that's precisely where the country of his birth finds itself.

He'd been quickly accepted by the Army and, within two weeks, found himself on a transport heading for Hawaii. The US Army Air Corps needed an evaluation of the damage done to its planes and airfields after the devastation of Pearl Harbor—and turned to the combat expertise of this 24-year-old pilot—a heady position for him to be in. The US military was still shell-shocked and needed something much more specific than estimates from state-side engineers and mechanics. He was one of several recruited to test the planes— but, in his mind, this placed him in a position of importance. At 24, that can be a perilous position for the ego.

The flight tests had gone well on the planes that hadn't been destroyed, although he'd rubbed a few of the older officers and NCOs' the wrong way. However, the younger pilots—already war-weary from the massive attack—thoroughly admired his no-nonsense approach to bureaucratic red tape.

No one seems to grasp what kind of trouble we're in; he reflects as he enters the officer's club. We're on an island in the middle of an ocean; there's no fleet to speak of; the Army is limited; and planes are, at a minimum, way beyond critical. Yep, I can't think of a better mess to be in, he concludes as the righteousness of youth creeps into his smile.

With that, he heads directly for the bar.

Chapter 15 ⌁ Mixed Signals

Sitting with a captain who's too eager to get his opinion on everything, he looks up just in time to see her walk in. He catches his breath. The only impression overtaking his now feeble brain: Oh my God—I've been hit by lighting!

As she walks toward her date, Captain Leonard Abrams, her eyes immediately divert to the man beside him. Instantly, an unrecognizable and, in her mind, an utterly unjustifiable wave of relief *and* anger sweep over her. By the time Leonard introduces them, both he and she can barely utter a coherent response. In fact, the whole conversation during the meeting of this dynamic duo doesn't go much better.

With great flair, Leonard stands up, "Alexa, this is Lt. John Eugene Conner, pilot extraordinaire. John, this is Alexandra O'Malley, a reporter for the New York Daily News; I might say she's getting quite a bit of attention."

Having stood immediately upon her approach, Jack extends his hand, barely waiting for Leonard to finish his introduction. Reaching to shake his hand—and with every bit of breeding she could muster—she acknowledges him, "Hello, John."

"No, it's Jack; short for John, which is my father's name." Smiling, he releases her hand and adds, "And may I call you Alex?"

Irritated by shortening her name to that which only those she cares about can call her, she replies, "No, you may call me Alexa. It's my professional name, and it's already short for Alexandra."

And so, it went for the rest of the uncomfortable conversation.

Leonard had ordered a round of drinks for the three of them, but it soon became apparent that this tall, striking man with a touch of silver sprinkled through his dark hair is almost invisible to the couple in front of him. As he watches the two of them awkwardly attempt to resist the powerful force that's pulling them together, Leonard silently laughs. At the ripe old age of 30, he's lived long enough to recognize that fighting an undeniable attraction—as overwhelming as it may be—never ends well. As Leonard takes the last sip of his drink, he wonders why destiny has propelled these two young creatures toward each other. Wistfully concluding that such musings are the poet inside him talking, Leonard immediately vows not to let feelings sway him from his mission at hand: There's too much resting on my shoulders. Whatever's happening in front of me with these two charming things, will have to be sacrificed—or destroyed.

With that, Leonard indicates he has a reservation for Alex and himself at the restaurant next door. Both she and Jack seem almost relieved to bring this meeting to an end. Taking her elbow as she gets up, Leonard shakes hands with Jack, almost feeling sorry for this arrogant, charming pilot. "We need to continue our chat soon, lieutenant."

"Oh sure . . . of course," Jack responds and looks over to someone entering the bar who catches his attention. Relieved by the distraction of feeling like a complete fool—something to which he is highly unaccustomed—Jack waves Steve over to them. Steve is the lead engineer from California who preceded Jack's arrival by a few weeks and one of the few engineers Jack can count on to have his back.

Quickly moving towards them but still several feet away, Steve calls out boisterously, "Well, two of my favorite people!" Slapping Jack on the back and putting a strong arm around Alex, Steve laughingly announces, "Wow, Alex, I didn't know you knew this rogue pilot! I'd be careful if I were you." Replying quickly with a stilted laugh, Alex takes advantage of the moment to introduce Steve to Leonard.

Still stunned that his new best friend is calling her *Alex*, Jack tries to smile as he asks Steve, "How long have you two known each other?"

"Oh, we've been fast friends for what . . . a good month now, right Alex?" Immediately sensing where this is going, Leonard joins in, "War makes all good friendships 'immediate'—time is a luxury now." With that, he again takes Alex's arm and apologizes for leaving. "Sorry, chaps, you know how damn hard these reservations are to get. The place next door is one of the few remaining restaurants open for dinner."

As Leonard and Alex move swiftly through the crowded bar towards the door, Jack's eyes never stop watching her. Still, in a bit of a haze, he turns to Steve with the comment, "Well, that was . . . interesting." Having never seen Jack at a loss for words before, a slight frown forms on Steve's face as he waves to the nearby bartender. Putting a hand on his friend's shoulder, he instructs, "Sit down, buddy, I think you need to fill me in."

Although sharing a lot in a few short weeks, deeply personal feelings had been limited between the two men; war does that to you. But both read each other very well. As the bartender starts to pour, he looks up at Steve—who responds to the unasked question, "Make it doubles."

Chapter 16 ᔆ The Conspiracies of War

"So, you think there's some dark conspiracy," Leonard asks, "with all the aircraft carriers being out at sea?" Having just left the restaurant, Alex and Leonard are walking towards the beach. Only the moon lights their way. "Are you saying that the President of the United States withheld information vital to keeping hundreds of people from being slaughtered? *Let alone* putting us behind the eight-ball by allowing most of our fleet to be destroyed?"

"I'm not saying that . . . out loud."

"Look, missy . . . you're getting dangerously close to something that's *way* beyond your paygrade. I don't care how much you feel the public has a 'right to know.' The carnage you see on the shore and floating in the sea means we're in a war like *no one* has ever seen before; holding back on a few 'rights' of the American public might save their lives."

"Wow, now that's a slippery slope."

"Yes, it is. But let me ask you this. Hypothetically, let's say the President and the Secretary of State knew 12 hours before that the Japs were going to war."

"Stop! How would they know that . . . hypothetically?!"

"Because they decoded the final telegram to the Japanese Ambassador in Washington. But they had no information on what kind of action the attack would be . . . or 'where' specifically, or even 'when.' And frankly, any analysis of the information would have put Pearl Harbor way down on the list."

"And you know this hypothetical fact how?"

"Let's just say I was close to the information in DC."

"Gee, now I think you'll tell me this is off the record."

"Way off. And you can bet your life on that."

"Careful now, or I'll figure you're being literal," she replies, half-smiling.

Silence is his response. Then, he turns to her, "Come on, let's go down to the water." He carefully looks around to ensure they're not being followed while helping her over the small wall separating the beach from the road.

As they reach a spot where the waves are gently riding up on the sand, he sits and helps her down beside him. Finally, he speaks.

"So, to continue. Do you really believe that 'if' our fleet here in Hawaii had been put on high alert and had been attacked, but driven off—the American people wouldn't want war with Japan?"

"Well, if you were in DC before Pearl Harbor, you saw the protesters on the White House lawn. They vehemently wanted nothing to do with the 'mess over there.' Leonard, you can't tell me that Roosevelt wasn't looking for a way into the war. It was only this past Thanksgiving that Churchill threatened him with retaliation for carrying Germans on a passenger ship!"

"Alexa, please. Put your reporter's hat away and use your God-given common sense. Wouldn't a successful defense of Pearl Harbor have made FDR look good? If an American ship had spotted the Japanese fleet headed towards Honolulu 'by chance,' did FDR plan to say, 'please just ignore those Japanese carriers; it's supposed to be a surprise.'"

Silence again. Only crashing waves are heard.

Alex speaks quietly, "Why are you telling me this?"

"Well, missy . . . that I also can't tell you. Not yet. Maybe not ever."

She realizes this is a turning point for her, but pieces are missing that she can't push for. "I still don't understand. But, okay."

"Just know for now, especially in your position, that it's important that you see that the enemy is not our government. Free as we all are, bureaucracy is fallible; human beings are fallible. And you're right; we should have known better, been better alerted. What happened here in Hawaii may happen to California—at any time—and we have little defense."

She looks at him directly. "So, you're only speaking to me because I'm a reporter?"

"No. Not only. I've watched you and how you handle yourself since you arrived."

"We didn't 'just meet by chance,' did we?"

"You mean you didn't 'influence' me to ask you out?"

"Something like that."

"No. I made sure we met. But I'm leaving Hawaii in a few hours, and there's little chance I'll see you for quite a while."

She starts to speak, but he briefly silences her with his finger across her lips. "No more questions, Alex. For now, remember that the actual enemy is the bully and the coward who brutally attacked us at daybreak. And although we rattled our sword from the sidelines, we were not at war with them or anybody."

"Seems they took their cue from Hitler."

"Yes," he responds as he helps her off the sand, "and now it's us against them *all*. God help us."

Chapter 17 ❧ Fate Steps In

T he island at dawn remains peaceful until you look away from the sunrise to the wreckage that's still scattered everywhere. Two months after the attack on Pearl Harbor, the island's beauty is a paradox to the devastation now a part of everyday life. The harbor is no longer littered with bodies, but the remaining wreckage of the ships is a continual reminder of the thousands of lost lives.

And no matter how many revisions to her stories Alexa has sent via the wire services, the censorship remains harsh. She's frustrated and restless, feeling her contribution is non-existent. The only attention she's getting is because she's a rare breed: a female reporter in the heart of a historic moment on the battlefield of war. But being a woman reporter is of no significance to her if she can't tell the story that exists around her. Fluff pieces about the heroic people entrenched in this mess are essential, of course. But not nearly as important to Alex as the consequences of this monumental attack in relationship to the destruction the enemy accomplished. Leonard is wrong; the public does have a *right to know* where we stand as a nation and what we must sacrifice if we're going to survive.

At the airfield, Jack and the others brought in to test the planes and get them up to fighting speed are now only days away from signing off on this unprecedented assignment. For weeks, all he could think of was going where he could cause the same kind of monstrous trouble in the air that his homeland faced on

December 7th. Anywhere he can retaliate is okay with him. And the sooner, the better.

As the day was coming to a close, Jack decides to take off one last time for one of his favorite places . . . the north shore. Flying low over the center of the island, he relishes the peace and the beauty of the dense jungle, broken only by the few pineapple plantations dotting the land. Typically, the north end is empty of human activity, except for the loyal young surfers who come here to test their skills in the life-threatening waves.

Approaching the north shore, Jack flies as low as he can, anticipating the rush of breaking away from the land and swinging out over the ocean for his return trip back to Pearl Harbor. On an isolated road a few hundred feet off a wide sandy beach, he sees a jeep stopped with the hood up, and someone bent over the engine. It had been a fairly calm day, and only a small group of surfers were clustered in the ocean, awaiting the non-existent waves.

The sun's going down quickly, and Jack realizes that the stranded person below has no way to be helped if the jeep can't be started. As he flies over the jeep, he tips his wings. The driver looks up, and Jack can see her face. The only thing that goes through his mind is that fate has a perverse sense of humor.

Landing easily on the beach, Jack quickly secures the plane out of harm's way and heads into the jungle to the awaiting jeep. This time in this isolated setting—cut off from any world they know or understand—there is no awkwardness.

"Well, small world; fancy meeting you here," Jack opens with as he approaches Alex.

"Somehow, I was expecting something a little more creative from you, based on our unique setting," she smiles back.

"Aha! This is as innovative as I get, being a simple man of the world," he retorts as he bends over to look into the engine.

A few minutes later, Alex is in the driver's seat, awaiting Jack's instructions. He has his flight jacket off, and his short sleeve uniform leaves his arms unprotected as he reaches deep into the engine. "Okay, let her rip." As she turns over the engine, she sees a stream of fire running up Jack's left arm. Alex's out of the jeep before Jack can say "shit!"—immediately followed with the string of profanities he recites as fast as he can say them. He drops and rolls on the ground as she grabs his jacket and smothers the fire on his hand and arm.

They both look at each other, then at the jeep, which is now purring beautifully. The ridiculousness of it all hits them as they start to laugh.

"We've got to get you treated. Your arm doesn't look too bad, but that hand is nasty," Alex comments as she tries to help Jack up."

"I don't suppose you know how to fly a plane," Jack responds with a half-smile.

"Sure, I can fly. I just can't take off or land yet," is her quick retort. "But I do know how to drive the jeep, so why don't you just get in and someone can deal with the plane later."

"Oh, I can't tell you how happy that's going to make my commander," Jack laments as he gets into the jeep's passenger side.

Alex moves the jeep onto the narrow road and steps on the gas. As she shifts into second gear and the wind starts blowing her hair, she answers, "Don't you worry, I'll write a nice little article about how you and the guys are the 'hidden saviors of Pearl Harbor' with all the work you've done. And . . . what an *absolute* gentleman you are in rescuing a damsel in distress. The military's going to love it!"

Chapter 18 ∽ Assignment California

"Excuse me, *sir* . . . what do you mean I'm going to California!?!" Jack is sitting in his Commander's office on the base at Oahu; his hand is still bandaged. Before his Commander can reply, Jack stands abruptly and loudly comments, "The enemy's not in California . . . yet . . . unless there's something you haven't told me."

"No, but Hollywood is. And that's where they're having a major war bond drive." Before Jack can respond, the Commander tells Jack to sit down and then continues. "And since Hollywood is our biggest propaganda machine, that's where you're going to be . . . *especially* now that you're a recognized symbol of the work we're all doing to fight this damn war."

"Sir, that article was about everyone here . . . I was barely mentioned. And my hand is almost healed, I can fly by next week. Please don't do this to me."

"Jack, be real. The article was great for all of us, but you were the face of it. And Alex did a fine job of pulling all the right stuff out of you and making it live. Rescuing her wasn't a bad ending, either. Just what the country needed to read."

The Commander stands, and Jack does the same, pleading, "Sir . . ."

"Jack, let's just consider this a good repayment for taking one of our valuable planes off for a joy ride and leaving it on a north shore beach." He looks at the inconsolable expression on Jack's face. "Oh, come on now. You'll only be gone for two weeks, and then I'll make sure you're assigned to someplace where you can throw yourself at the bloody enemy."

"What do you *mean* I'm going to California!?!" Alex is standing next to Charles. He's her very prim and proper Samoan friend sitting at his desk at Army's Intelligence headquarters, while Alexa is using his secure phone. Charles has a hard time not smiling as he hears Alex's side of the conversation with her editor, Fred, at the New York Daily News.

"*Dear Jehoshaphat Fred,* this is getting ridiculous! I'm a highly capable reporter who has now seen more than most men on your payroll . . . I'm *not* eye candy!"

Silence.

"Of course, I know this is important for the war effort . . . yes, I'm aware that the article had a nice impact . . . okay, okay, a strong impact . . . but if you just let me report some of what we're all facing here . . . no, I *don't* want to come home!"

Silence.

"Wait, Fred . . . you owe me! I've sent some great stuff from here . . . just because you . . . .*Fred?* . . . Fred!"

Alex drops her hand with the phone in it and turns to Charles. "Well, I'll be damned. He told me that the official papers were processed, and plans made and to make the best of it. Then he hung up."

Charles no longer tries to hide his laugh. "Well, just look at it this way, Alex, maybe you'll get lucky, and the Japs will attack Hollywood while you're at the Canteen." He laughs out loud now.

"Funny. And Fred would probably want me to disguise it as a bad earthquake. He's so pissed at the government censors, but still, he yields." She sits glumly in the chair facing Charles' desk. "You're the one with all the info; what chance do I have of seeing any action on the coast of California."

"Honey, if I had that kind of information, we wouldn't have been attacked here in the first place. But I sympathize. There's a group starting up in Alabama for colored military who want to be pilots. It's called the Tuskegee project. I've applied, but my bosses keep overriding me. Seems I do my job here *too well*, but I'll keep trying."

"So, a Samoan from Hawaii is considered colored in the US?"

"Yes indeed. Especially when your mother, who is a nurse, is colored and born in California."

"Ah, so true love is what brought her here so long ago! How do your parents feel about you flying?"

Taking a deep breath, Charles responds as a wistful look comes across his face, "Ohhhh . . . that's a long story."

"Great, we can compare parent stories over lunch—and I bet I can outdo you." With that, Charles stands up and gives her his arm. Alex wraps her arm in his. Smiling, she quickly adds, "Your treat!"

Chapter 19 ❧ Los Angeles

Los Angeles, California:

The military transport lands without a hitch on the long runway a mile from the Pacific Ocean in Los Angeles. With several runways and a single terminal building, it's a large airport in the middle of nowhere surrounded by orange, lemon, and grapefruit trees whose scents continually permeate the winter air. Looking north, a small mountain range runs from the ocean on east as far as the eye can see.

Military personnel exit the plane via the steep portable steps on the tarmac, with Alexa and Jack being the last to leave. Standing at the top of the stairs, the two of them look out towards the mountains where white stucco houses and red-tile roofs dot the landscape amongst a variety of trees and flowers.

"Well, it's a lovely city . . . if that's what you can call it, with no buildings higher than a three-story house," Alex comments as she shields her eyes with her hand from the sharp afternoon sun.

"Okay. I see that no matter how much the girl leaves New York, you definitely can't take New York out of the girl," Jack replies, looking further east across the mountain range. "I think that Hollywood is tucked into the foothills over there."

"Well, let's get this over with . . . you get to do your Joe Fly-Boy song and dance, and I'll tell the world how fine young men like you will save Western civilization."

"Isn't that a little too much pressure to put on a war bond tour?" Jack responds, taking Alex's elbow as they descend the airplane's stairs. "And besides, you built the image; now we're both stuck with it."

Her smile comes easily, which surprises her. "It's not such a bad image. Remember, Jack, I don't make up the news; I just record it for history."

"Oh, I see; now I'm a historic relic! Well, that's it; I'm heading back before I'm too old to fight." His laugh is comfortable, and his hand is still placed gently in the small of her beautifully curved back as they cross the tarmac to the terminal building.

The California sun catches the highlights of his thick dark blond hair. In that instant, she looks up at him to respond, only to find a momentary catch in her throat. With their bodies still close together as they walk, he immediately senses an almost imperceptible difference in her stride. His eyes lock briefly with hers. Breaking the effect his gaze has produced in her, she looks away and responds with, "Ah, come on. It's all for the sake of getting the public to buy enough bonds so we can afford to kill the enemy. Be a good sport."

"You're right; we both got ourselves into this mess. Celebrities, a little R & R . . . might as well enjoy this visit in the land of milk and honey," he retorts. With that, he opens wide the terminal door and does a half-bow as she sweeps past him. She doesn't see her skirt gently wave near his face, leaving only the slightest hint of her perfume behind. Holding tight onto the terminal door as he comes up from his bow—he takes a split second to recover.

Chapter 20 ✑ War Bond Tour

T he Southern California Spanish Revival architecture wows them both. Nothing in England or on the East Coast prepares them for the beauty this unique city—one that lazily stretches for miles inland from the sea. The art deco buildings are clean, gleam brightly, and surrounded by a variety of tall palms.

Homes with red tile roofs and gleaming white walls are covered with vibrant bougainvillea, while the fragrance of honeysuckle permeates everywhere. Sometimes, on a clear and star-filled night, a waft of the ocean air carried by a soft California wind can be detected, if only for a few seconds. And the weather—unlike Hawaii—has cool evenings vacillating with the warmth of the days, with little of that humidity that can wring the life out of you.

They start their journey up and down the state from the new Union train station in downtown Los Angeles. They're on a bond tour from San Francisco to San Diego that takes them from early morning to late into the evening for over a week. Each city, town, or suburb in this sprawling state they face eager and enthusiastic crowds. Jack and Alexa's youth and personal stories give a face to the war effort but most importantly, provide hope to a nation still reeling from a major attack. They help raise millions for a military that's more on the drawing board than built in the form of tanks, ships, and planes. But by the week's end, both Alexa and Jack are happy to be finishing up in Los Angeles for their final parade.

By now, an easy friendship has formed between the two. With so many questions thrown at them wherever they go on the tour, they automatically seem to have each other's back. Only some questions are allowed to be answered, and only then within the strictest of parameters. And no matter how tired they are, they're expected to chat continually, building enthusiasm to face a war on two fronts while saying nothing of importance. War is the subject of their work, but it's far from their minds when they're alone—so laughter comes easily and often.

On the long train rides, they share stories about their up-bringing, and each is privately surprised to find how vulnerable they'd become with the other. Soon, they find themselves at their last stop—back in the magic land of Los Angeles. With all that they've accomplished, it seems like a month since they first arrived. Although the city is still concerned about the enemy landing on its coast and blackouts are standard nightly, they're treated like royalty. Hollywood definitely knows how to party—even in the face of war.

Chapter 21 ❦ Hollywood Canteen

The Hollywood Canteen is filled with service members of every rank from every branch, and all are welcomed as stars serve food and drinks to those who may never return. For now, there's abundant laughter mixing with music, smoke, and the smell of pungent liquors.

Hedy Lamarr approaches a table where Alex and Jack are entertained by several actors, their girlfriends, and a small group of militaries assigned to them as escorts—one young, attractive WAVE and two ensigns. The men all stand as one of Hollywood's most attractive celebrities joins them. "Oh, sit down, everyone, please," Hedy retorts, wavering her beautiful hand sparkling with bright red nail polish,

The stunning redhead doesn't sit but leans her hands on the table, hoping the honored guests can hear her with all the surrounding noise. "My, what a busy day! You sure wowed them. And you two looked great sitting together on the back of the red convertible coming down Hollywood Boulevard—what a parade! But your speech at the podium, Jack, describing what Hawaii's like right now, brought us all to tears."

"Well, thank you. But it was Alex who really helped me form my ideas. She's the creative one. I just fly planes for a living."

"Don't listen to him, Miss Lamarr. Those planes will save a lot of lives," Alex immediately jumps in, leaning into Hedy.

"Call me Hedy, please, Alexa. I agree, but I've read your stuff, young lady . . . it's obvious you're also doing your part."

"Well, I'm trying to, I . . . "

"I know," Hedy cuts her off. "We're all doing our part in whatever way we can; not always easy." And, with a quick wink, she continues, "I hope we have a chance to talk in the future." With that, Hedy takes her hands off the table and announces loudly to Jack and Alex, "Okay, you two—you look too good together not to be taking center stage in the middle of that dance floor. Get out there."

With too much noise and activity in the canteen to protest, Jack looks at Alex and raises his eyebrow, and a slight smile crosses his face as he offers his hand. "Oh, why not . . . it's for the war effort," she replies as they stand and head for the dance floor.

The dance area is large but packed with bodies, especially now that a lingering ballad is playing *Ebb Tide*. Carving out a little space for them to move gently, Jack puts his arm around Alex's waist and pulls her in tight. She folds into him beautifully as she places her arm securely around his neck and across his shoulder. When she looks up at him, their lips practically touch—something the rest of their bodies have already accomplished. The smell of her engulfs him, while the feel of his muscles moving as he holds her ripples through every fiber of her body. Winter in Los Angeles: it's cool outside, but inside there's nothing but intense heat in the small space that only they occupy with their bodies and *Ebb Tide*.

The music ends, but quickly the band picks up with a boogie-woogie, and the drums go wild. Jack and Alex have dropped their arms but, for mere seconds, are unable to move away from each other. Hedy Lamarr has reached them, immediately grabbing their attention by pushing a card into Jack's hand. She nods, and they follow her off the floor and out the canteen door.

"That card is your introduction to the concierge. I will have already called him while your escort takes you over to the Sunset Tower." Jack and Alexa are looking at Hedy with an unspoken question in their eyes. "Look," she continues, "I know you're at the Hollywood Roosevelt Hotel—which is fine and quite popular with parties going all night long. But some important friends maintain a suite at this gorgeous new apartment complex on the Sunset Strip. I think you'll be very impressed."

"Thank you, Hedy, so much. But we're okay at . . . " Alex tries to express her reservation.

"Of course, you are, but that's not the point! And you two should experience this new art deco building. It's a landmark, except for city hall, the tallest in town. You'll enjoy the view, Alex, if you've been missing your hometown."

On Alex's look, Hedy continues, "And, it's a two-bedroom penthouse. I wouldn't dare compromise either of you while you're serving our nation with such honor." Hedy allows only a slight smile on her gorgeous red lips.

Jack takes it as a gift of appreciation and reaches for Hedy's hand to shake it. "Thank you. We sincerely mean it."

Hedy laughs and reaches to kiss him on the cheek, then does the same to Alex. "You're certainly welcome. Now, see that Pontiac sedan over there? That cute WAVE will drive you to the Sunset Tower; she knows LA like the back of her hand. She'll probably regale you with a few stories as you drive there. Frankly, I think she's been in every bar and restaurant along the way. The Tower's less than 15 minutes from here, but in that short distance, some pretty colorful history has been made."

Chapter 22 ∾ Leaving the World Behind

L eaving the brightly lit corridor of nightlife behind on the Sunset Strip, the car pulls off of the Strip and into the sweeping entrance of the grand and opulent Sunset Tower. Immediately, the doorman opens the backseat car door and welcomes them. "We've been expecting you. Your luggage arrived a while ago and is already in your suite, so your check-in with the concierge will be brief."

"Well, that answers my first question," Alexa comments as the doorman offers her a hand to help her out. Sliding over to exit, Jack lowers his voice so only the driver can hear, "Isn't that interesting; our luggage arrived before we accepted the invitation." To which the driver, the WAVE junior officer, Mage, replies, "They are difficult people to say no to, sir."

As the doorman shuts the car door, he winks at Mage and observes, "You sure look cute tonight."

"Thanks, Harry," she replies as she puts the car into first gear, "but you're just a sucker for a uniform." And, with a return wink, she leaves.

The double doors open wide as Jack and Alex enter the penthouse, where only a few mood lights highlight the living room. The apartment is appointed beautifully, but the view in front of them commands their immediate attention. The Sunset Tower is only 18 stories high, but since they're at the highest point in the tallest building for as far as they can see, they feel they're on top of the world—and alone. Los Angeles at night is crystal clear, with the city's lights twinkling endlessly as they stretch past downtown, miles away.

After Jack closes and locks the suite's doors, he moves across the room and joins Alexa. She's standing at the two-story windows as Jack walks up and gently puts his hand on her shoulder. The electricity of his touch makes her body jolt.

"Oh, I'm sorry; I didn't mean to startle you. I just wanted to direct your attention to the left."

Alexa looks in that direction and can see a plane landing in the distance. Just beyond that, as the coastline curves, the lights disappear, and blackness takes over. "Oh, that must be the ocean in that direction," she comments.

"Yes, he replies gently, "I'll bet it's a beautiful site at sunrise."

She laughs and turns to look at him. "You do know, of course, that the sun sets over the ocean here."

"Yes, I think I know my east from west," he smiles wide. "But with all the buildings being so low in Los Angeles, the sun streams right on through to the beach as it rises . . . Miss Smarty Pants."

"Ahh . . . something New York doesn't have! With buildings fighting for space in the sky, that's something we never see. *Very* observant, Jack."

"Thank you! I've been told I'm a very observant person. It helps in my line of work."

"Well, I'd say that's an attribute you've cultivated in all areas of your life," Alexa comments.

"Interesting; it sounds like you have something specific in mind. Wanta share?"

"The night we met," Alexa comments quietly as she turns back to the carpet of lights out the massive window.

"Oh . . . that night. *The* night. I hadn't thought of it as 'observing.' But we can go with that."

"From the moment I entered the bar."

"I didn't think you noticed from that far away."

"You're pretty powerful, sir. . . I think I felt you before I saw you."

Jack's standing very close, right behind Alexa now. They're both still looking at the night's magic before them.

"Well, you knocked any sense out of me from the moment you started coming towards us. When I realized you were the date Leonard was waiting for, part of me jumped for joy inside, and the other part looked for a place to hide." This time, when he puts his hand softly on her shoulder, she leans into him slightly. His voice is now very low. "Why were you so angry with me when we met."

She hesitates, takes a small breath, and answers. "Because I felt you could see into my soul by just looking at me. I'd . . . I'd never experienced that . . . no one has ever done that to me; I guess it scared me."

He turns her around gently, and once again, their bodies are touching completely. Sliding his arms around her waist, she places her arms around his neck.

"I was vulnerable in a way I've never been," she continues.

"As was I." he whispers, his lips moving down over hers.

Their lips caress, and the kiss crescendos, releasing a flood of emotions within. With no conscious effort, their bodies move in harmony . . . while their minds connect in a language only they understand. They know what they want; they know what the other needs.

At every point of contact, their bodies now surrender to the feelings consuming them. The rapture grows.

His touch once again burns her skin as he finds her breast, pleasure rippling through her body. Reaching down, she finds him—and, in doing so, takes his breath away. Her gentle touch is searing and moves him to an emotional pitch that's both unrelenting and unparalleled with anything he's ever known.

In that moment, he knows he'll never get enough of her—and there will never be enough time, no matter how long his body clings to hers.

With their bodies still wrapped within each other, he gently lifts Alex, still enfolded in his arms. Almost floating, he moves them to the oversized silk couch only a few feet from the massive window.

Hungry for each other, their bodies move even closer until each breath they take seems like one. Neither is anxious to hurry—a rhythmic dance unfolds that they seem to have done before—compelling them to experience it now as new and undiscovered.

Each movement is savored, no matter how small. The pain of the slow release is exquisite, one that they welcome with total surrender. The completion of their fusion together is something they've been waiting for—for a long, long time.

It's here on this luxurious couch bathed in the lights of the city that they explore each other until dawn's first rays find them. And then, with the warmth of the early sun streaking their bodies, they're given over to a new height.

A soul finding a mate . . . with not even air between them.

And two beautiful bedrooms go unused.

The next 12-hour time frame is a blur. They sleep when necessary and then only for the briefest of time. Instinctively, each knows that every moment must be explored and discovered again and again.

There's an urgency that neither understands. An undercurrent both feel but never mention.

Chapter 23 ❧ Dawn's New Path

A phone, somewhere in the distance, is ringing.

Somehow, dusk has started to show itself—entering the oversized window and slowly darkening the penthouse once again. Jack reaches for the phone, somewhat amazed that he found it on the first try; he isn't sure which bedroom they are now in. Hedy's unmistakable voice is clear and on the edge of being boisterous.

"Well, your first day off to rest. Did you have a great day? Exploring the city, I hope."

Jack smiles as he strokes Alex's hair draped across his pelvis. "Well, we did a lot of exploring but stayed around this area."

"Ah, I see. No doubt you put it to good use. Well, now that the bond tour is over, a friend of mine wants you two to be guests for the weekend at his summer home. There's going to be a grand party, and he wants you to meet some people."

Jack sits up and tries to orient himself. The idea of Alex and he sharing these last few hours of privacy with anyone else sends a cold chill down his back. "Hedy, that's lovely. But we've been gone for 12 days; the transport is taking off tomorrow night for Hawaii—and I have orders to be on it."

"Don't be silly darling, that's been all taken care of. I think the Army can get along without you for a few more days. Everyone's dying to meet you, and your ace reporter definitely can't miss mingling with some of the people who will be attending. To say it would be good for her career is an understatement."

"Well, I guess it's all decided then."

"Of course, it is," Hedy responds with a smile in her voice.

Jack slides back down, holding Alex's naked body with one arm as she moves her body up and tucks it into his. "Hedy, does anyone ever get to say no to you?"

"Let me think . . . no, sweetheart, I don't think I've had that experience."

Jack laughs. He's brought the gold and white phone receiver to his other shoulder so Alex can listen.

"By the way, I had my Roadster convertible dropped off with your valet about an hour ago," Hedy cheerfully continues. "There are directions on how to get to the summer home in the glove box. I thought a leisurely drive up our beautiful coast tomorrow would add to your memories. It's magnificent scenery."

Jack and Alex smile at each other as they continue to listen.

"Tomorrow night's casual, so if you're there by late afternoon, you two can take a dip in the pool before the BBQ. The big party's the next night."

"Hedy, you still haven't mentioned who our host will be," Jack adds.

"Oh, silly me! It's the newspaper tycoon William Randolph Hearst. You'll drive to his home in San Simeon; Hearst Castle."

As Jack wraps up his call with Hedy, Alex sits up straight and remains with her mouth half-open.

Chapter 24 ∽ The Coast North

Looking over at her as the wind blows through her hair, Jack feels his heart start to race all over again. Taking one hand off the wheel, he gently slips it up her leg, under her skirt, and quickly tucks his fingers into her panties. Feeling her moisture on his fingertips would have caused an accident if they'd been anywhere other than on the nearly isolated Highway 1. The coast highway runs the length of the state, paralleling the Pacific Ocean, which is often only a few yards away from the road. The little convertible Roadster is in perfect sync with the flow of the coastline—and for the couple inside, time has stopped entirely. In their universe, there's no tomorrow, only now.

Making it up the coast easily, they swing off the highway and through the gates of Hearst Castle about an hour before the first streak of sunset.

The hardest part of the drive was getting on the road in the first place. Leaving the penthouse meant leaving the privacy of their own paradise—where finding each other had been like coming home after a long trip. Looking from room to room of the suite, they saw the effects of their lovemaking – each bedroom and even the living room again had become their domain. As they stood with their luggage near the apartment door, surveying the chaos one more time, they looked at each other and laughed.

"Where did the time go," she asks, with a glow still radiating from her whole face. "After the first kiss . . . I have no idea," he responds, giving her one more lingering brush across her lips. Then, he quickly opens the door for them to leave.

Chapter 25 ❧ Hearst Castle

Resting on 240,000 acres in San Simeon, California, Hearst Castle leaves them both speechless when they walk through the main house doors. An unusual combination of hanging tapestries and art, unique-hand painted tile work, artifacts, and full beams and staircases of hand-carved wood from almost every major "kingdom" in Europe dresses the summer home. The only thing truly American is the everyday furniture, the owner, newspaper magnate William Randolph Hearst, and his mistress, movie star Marion Davies. Marion is actually the belle of the ball and the one all events are centered around.

Hedy greets Jack and Alex with her warm welcome. She introduces them to an impressive and eclectic group of business, political, and entertainment luminaries—all seeming to have great wit and charm in common. Soon they're sweeping through the massive living room, following the butler up the ornately carved staircase to the second floor, where they're shown their bedrooms, which just happened to be next to each other. Happily noticing their proximity, Jack winks at Alexa as each enters their respective bedrooms to quickly unpack and change for the pool.

After wandering the grounds to take in the menagerie of animals that reside on the estate, they find the indoor pool and spend a delightful hour swimming with several high-profile guests. The large, Olympic-size pool is beautifully decorated with hand-painted Italian tiles among gold inlaid tiles from India. For the two lovers, this is a surreal world far from the madness of war and destruction.

Marion Davies is a charming hostess, ensuring that everyone has whatever they need during cocktail hour. The piano player entertains without interruption, and the conversations flow easily. However, 15 minutes before dinner, all the liquor is cleared away out of respect for the owner descending the stairs to join his guests. William Hearst does not believe in the sin of alcohol—and sees no reason why his guests would.

A light California rain begins to fall as the two dozen guests dine in the "Refectory" at one long table. This is a rare and exclusive combination of people, all familiar to each other without having met. Away from the limelight, the conversations are pretty lively as new acquaintances become fast friends.

Shortly after dinner, as Marion and William move everyone toward the theater to watch the latest movie, Jack slips his hand into Alex's and quietly guides her away from the crowd, up the staircase towards the bedrooms.

The rains beat all night long. The heavy drops pounding a surface like an orchestra will always remind Alexa and Jack of this night . . . of this dance . . . of the heat and passion that drives them, again and again, to be consumed by each other. As their bodies slide gracefully across each other, every movement of their dance will instantly be recalled as the rain plays music to their lovemaking. With an intense heat pulsing within him, Jack slowly plunges himself inside her as she reaches up to become a part of his body. Once again, they find the echo of a deep familiarity that will haunt them forever.

Chapter 26 ᗢ Spies Among Us

T hey awake to the California sun once again, warming their naked bodies as they lie entwined on the bed. The realization of where they are drives them to get up and dress and to move towards downstairs as quickly as possible, knowing they're expected for breakfast at 9 am.

The day rolls by with the beauty of the California winter turning into spring as they play tennis, swim, and then take a walk on the beach. In the late afternoon, the day turns cold with a brisk wind creating small white caps on the pounding surf. As they walk with arms wrapped around each other, they glance up into the hills. From the beach, they can easily see Hearst's castle in all its glory on the hill, rising like their own private Camelot beckoning them home.

Sun-burned and wind-swept, they enter the living room with plans to go immediately upstairs to prepare for the grand party. Cocktails are already being served for a few of the many guests that have arrived early, and across the room, leaning against the black grand piano, is Leonard, talking animatedly with Hedy. Looking tan in his dress blue Navy uniform, he holds a scotch and soda in his hand. Seeing the momentary shock on Alexa and Jack's faces, Hedy calls them over with a sweep of her arm, meeting them half-way across the massive living room. Her voice is low even though only about ten people are in the room, small groups all seemingly caught-up in their conversations.

"Ahh, the two lovebirds! Why don't the two of you go change, then join Leonard and me on the patio? The rest of the guests will be arriving any time."

"That's a great idea, Hedy," Jack responds, smiling broadly with his arm still around Alex. Then lowering his voice to almost a whisper, he continues. "And then, maybe then, he can explain how he left Hawaii as a Captain in the Army and arrived in California as a Commander in the Navy." Leonard winks at the two as they move past him on their way to the staircase. As soon as they're side-by-side, Alex smiles and says, "You're looking great, Leonard, so glad to see you . . . can't wait to hear what you've been up to since we last spoke."

Chapter 27 ᕤ OSS—The Reveal

T he sun has started its decline into the long California sunset, calming the winds that blow from the ocean. About 70
guests are mingling in the living room and flowing out onto the
grand patio, but Leonard and Hedy have found a somewhat private spot outside as Jack and Alexa approach them with drinks.
All too aware that whatever Leonard is up to, it's obviously a
wartime need-to-know. Jack looks around the enormous patio to
make sure no one's in earshot.

"Well, hello, Commander. You've certainly risen fast in the
ranks since Hawaii." To which Alexa adds, "And switched branches, I see . . . neat trick."

Leonard replies with his devilishly clever smile, "Let's take a
walk amongst the animals for a while, shall we? At least we know
that none of them are spies."

Once the four of them are within the grounds of the animals'
pens and find no trace of anyone else, Leonard stops, sips his drink,
and turns to his friends.

"Well, just the two people I wanted to see. Thank you, Hedy,
for arranging this."

"Darling, for you . . . and the war effort . . . anything." She
smiles coyly.

Alexa tilts her head and smiles. "Why am I beginning to feel
this was all set up long ago?"

"Oh, because it was, my sweet. At least as soon as Jack burnt his hand rescuing you and your jeep," Leonard grins with a certain sense of accomplishment.

"Are you kidding, Leonard?" Alexa responds, a bit dumbfounded. "You have that much clout to maneuver *everything* since then!?! Pulling me out of Hawaii . . . getting *Jack* reassigned for two weeks . . . putting us on tour . . . the canteen . . . the . . . the"

"Oh, the penthouse was my idea," Hedy interjects with a sly smile. "I certainly hope you enjoyed yourselves." With fresh memories lingering like a soft perfume, a slight blush has already started to move up Alexa's face.

"And while I can't take credit for Hearst having this party— Hedy did make sure you were on the guest list. It was the perfect time for all of us to rendezvous in a more 'secure' location." With that, Leonard downs the last of his highball.

"And William was quite happy with that. I must say, you two have made an excellent impression here," Hedy adds, her green eyes sparkling."

"Okay . . . down to brass tacks." Leonard starts to walk casually, making sure no one is around. They all follow his slow pace; Alexa and Jack are still slightly jarred by the machinations and the unknowing part they've played.

Once they settle into another secured spot, Hedy hands Leonard her drink saying, "You take this, dear; I think you're going to need another."

Len gratefully accepts her glass and takes the next few minutes to summarize where the world is at that moment—the actual reality of what they face.

"In Europe, the US has entered the war against German forces that now control Poland, Denmark, Norway, France, Luxembourg, the Netherlands, Belgium, Yugoslavia, and Greece. While this grand party is taking place here, in the paradise we call California, Germany is making an effective siege against the Soviet Union. Furthermore, Mussolini has plans to cede Trieste, South Tyrol, and Istria to Germany."

"So," he takes a deep breath and continues, "England, holding on by a thread, is now the last country left to fight the Nazis. She's completely cut off from all of her colonies—unable to protect vital countries that are ripe for the picking by the Japs, Germans, and even the dysfunctional Italians."

Jack and Alexa remain fixated on Leonard as he sips his scotch. Then . . . "I know you know most of this but let me just recap the Pacific theater for you—the worldwide reality is beyond startling."

After looking around for a moment, Leonard continues. "Japan's opening salvo was with the bombing of Pearl Harbor. As the dawn moved westward from Hawaii on across the Pacific that day . . . Japan laid waste to the US territories of Wake, Guam, and the Mariana Islands. These morning airstrikes on US military bases, initiated Japan's entrance into WWII. But as we all saw, that was only her opening gambit. The rest were there for her taking. On December 8th , the Japanese Imperial Navy attacked the U.S. Clark Field in the Philippines—a vital base and another unprecedented embarrassment—along with two other important Philippines' bases. They then finished with Manila—and lastly, for a tasty desert, took Thailand, Hong Kong, and Singapore. It was a tactical victory for Japan—capturing the Philippines was essential to the complete control of shipping routes between Japan and Greater East Asia."

Leonard downs the rest of his drink. "The upshot: If Germany conquers North Africa and Egypt, she can easily move on to capture the Suez Canal, meeting Japan on the other side. The war will be over. The Axis powers of Germany, Italy, and Japan will impenetrably control all the world's shipping lanes."

Hedy puts her hand gently on Leonard's arm. "It's time, dear, to get to the important part. He nods with a slight smile, then starts, "There's a new wartime intelligence organization, the OSS— the Office of Strategic Services. It's an agency of the Joint Chiefs of Staff to coordinate espionage activities behind enemy lines for all branches of the United States Armed Forces."

He has Alexa and Jack's attention—who are still holding their mostly untouched drinks. Leonard continues. "Other OSS functions included the use of propaganda and subversion. My job is to recruit—that's where you two come in. Thus, a different uniform for each base I visit. And, believe me, as a Jew, it suits me just fine to serve my country anywhere in official American territory."

Jack starts first. "My God, Len." Then silence, as Jack shakes his head. "Bravo."

Equally stunned, Alexa continues, "You're a part of this espionage ring, Hedy?"

"Yes, my dear. Many of us are—entertainers, writers, business leaders, and scientific advocates like Einstein. Oh, the list goes on. Wherever we can be of service—as you say, 'hiding in plain sight,'" she retorts. Her beautiful red lips slowly form an intriguing smile as she looks at Leonard. "Some of us can go behind enemy lines; some of us can't."

Leonard shares a brief, intimate smile with Hedy, then quickly pivots to Jack and Alex. "Ah! But you two can! Jack, you're being assigned to an aircraft carrier at Midway—our intel tells us that's the Japanese Navy's next likely target and will probably be our most important battle. We lose; we're finished. We can't be caught with our pants down as we were in Hawaii and the Philippines. Your CO will give you orders for you to communicate directly with me or someone of rank at OSS, whenever possible, of course."

"Well, hopefully, I'll be a little busy. What could I possibly give you that my CO can't?"

"The true lay of the land—without waiting weeks for us to get it through the damn military bureaucracy. Bits and pieces after the mop-up won't help us much in the next move forward."

Leonard tries to continue as Alexa interjects.

"So, the military isn't exactly fond of this new agency?"

"They're not fond of any extra government agency they have to account to," Leonard quickly answers. "God knows they have enough paperwork already. So, we're hoping to make it easier for them while they're trying to save the world, our country, and their men—along with their ships and planes."

"Len . . . I'll be fighting. All I can give you is what I see," Jack adds.

"And what you hear as well. What you see *and* what you hear . . . before, during, and immediately after any initiative you're in. You've been cleared. That goes for you too, Alex."

"Okay," she nods.

"Believe me, Jack, your assessments will help us coordinate espionage activities while the game is in play."

"Yeah, if I stay alive through this."

"Well, that *is* the hope."

For a moment, Alex and Jack look at each other. They're back in their own world and care not who's watching. Jack puts his arm tightly around the woman he now deeply loves and whispers, "Nothing's forever except us."

Solemnly she responds, "I know."

"And now, Alex, that leads us to you," Leonard continues, nodding to Hedy.

"Ahh, my area of expertise!" Hedy smiles graciously. "As my esteemed colleague said, the other OSS functions include the use of propaganda and subversion. In our case, it's an attack on the public morale—getting the general population to break loyalties to their political and social institutions."

"I see," Alex said. "Like French citizens fighting the French Vichy government. They call those rebels the 'French Underground,' from the rumors I've heard."

"You're right," Leonard answers, "and there's a growing resistance in Poland as well. But all that resistance is just getting traction and is vulnerable. We need an effective weapon—first, to keep up morale and then, to throw off our enemy."

Alex feels her old ire coming to the surface. "Okay. But the full-body censorship that's crippled our press since Pearl Harbor does nothing but make the public mad. The horror and the facts will eventually come out. Silence is not the answer."

"Ahh yes, my dear!" Hedy adamantly agrees. "We Americans are not stupid. We may have grown soft and enjoy our 'trinkets' too much, as our German 'friends' state . . . but we're still scamps and fighters."

"How true!" said Leonard. "So now we need to *bend* the obvious facts. And, like it or not, censorship coming from the US is still heavy, so we need a correspondent planted where the action is."

". . . wherever that may be," Hedy adds.

Leonard concludes. "And I will feed you bits of what I hear from Jack and the other men planted in both theaters. It's up to you to pull it all together for the papers."

"Okay, you've talked to the New York Daily News editor, *my boss?*"

"Yes," said Leonard. "He's not happy putting you in this position, but he's fed up with the censorship and, therefore, very reluctantly on board."

"Okay, fine. I'll go wherever you want—but the Daily News doesn't cover the whole country."

"No." Hedy is smiling. "But that, along with the Hearst newspaper chain—you've pretty much got total penetration."

Alex is staring in shock.

"Yes, dear, we're putting you in a very creme-de-la-creme position, one envied by correspondents twice your age. So, watch your back."

"Look, Alex," Leonard continues, "now that we're no longer 'neutral,' all of our correspondents have been escorted out from behind enemy lines. But with our network, you'll be in the thick of it all. And I know you can handle it. I told you as much that night on the beach in Hawaii."

"*But* you both have to understand," Hedy said, "this is strictly on a volunteer basis. We know it's asking a lot of you. Probably more than you realize, standing here under a California sky." She looks up waving her soft, beautiful hand, "Here . . . where the stars come out, making the world seem so splendid and innocent."

Deep twilight has fallen as the four have talked. From the merriment and music coming from the castle, no one seems to have missed them. Jack turns to Alex.

"Are you alright?"

"I don't know. But I know we have to do this."

"Right." Then Jack turns to Leonard. "No question about it."

"You both will deal directly with me, Hedy, or one of our superiors. The OSS is here to help conquer the enemy—and we're *way* behind. Most of our Navy is still on the drafting board. Factories all over America are being converted overnight for war production, and our countrymen are rising to the occasion handily. But frankly, America depends a lot on providence now—and we're just trying to help the gods along."

Leonard stands straighter and looks at both sternly.

"One more thing, then we'll leave you two alone. Do not automatically assume that you're among friends whenever you talk of the war and the direction this nation should move. You understand that while many of us are in great favor of Western civilization saving the world from cataclysmic tyranny, a few amongst us believe a dictatorship—be it a person or a committee—is the only way to govern a messy population. They're definitely not in the majority, but several are powerful."

With that, Leonard offers Hedy his arm and leads her back along the winding path, following the festive lights to the main house where the party is in full swing.

Still hidden by the darkness of the night, Jack takes Alex into his arms.

"We can do this."

"I know we can. I just don't want to lose you."

"You can't. You knew we're on borrowed time—but what time we've had is ours now . . . and forever." He kisses her softly and seductively. When they finish, their eyes stay locked. "And didn't you say that 'souls travel in packs?' You can't get rid of me."

She wrinkles up her nose as tears form in her eyes. "I don't care about the next life. Who really knows?!? I want you in this one!"

"We're doing this, Alex, so we actually get a chance to *have* a life, so *all* of us have a chance. You know this is what both of us always wanted . . . to make a difference. This world's gone insane—and first, we have to try, somehow, to fix it. Maybe it's what we're destined to do."

"What's that my daring flyer now says?!? I thought you had major doubts about *destiny*."

"Well, you just might have enlightened me." With that, a moment of pain creeps into his smile as they hold each other close in this idyllic setting—far from reality ahead of them.

Chapter 28 ᴄ And It Begins

The Battle of Midway (June 3rd–6th 1942):

A n important World War II naval battle fought almost entirely with aircraft. The US will destroy Japan's first-line carrier strength and most of her best-trained naval pilots. Hawaii is now safe from attack.

The goal of the attack on Pearl Harbor was to cripple the US Pacific Fleet and prevent it from intervening in Japan's planned seizure of resources and territories throughout the Pacific. Eight months later, Japan's goal of the attack on Midway is to extend Japan's now massive "absolute national defense zone" so the US can't mount hit and run carrier strikes like the Doolittle raid on Tokyo (April 1942). Also, Japan desperately wants a "decisive" battle with the remnants of the US Pacific Fleet—hopefully resulting in the US fleet's annihilation with the United States agreeing to a negotiated peace.

Even with heavy losses of precious human assets, the US wins the Battle of Midway without losing its vital carriers—and kicks off its island-hopping campaign in the Southwest and Central Pacific without risking the entire Pacific Fleet in a single battle. The tide might be turning.

As a fighter bomber pilot, Jack finds himself aboard an aircraft carrier in Midway, about a month before the Japanese attack that island. The US finally broke the Japanese code that indicates a scheduled time for the attack—early June 1942. This time, the U.S.

is prepared. Japan believes they have the element of "surprise" . . . but the United States is ready and lying in wait for her.

The two-day battle for Jack is bloody, exhausting, and rough. But his skills keep him alive—that and his consuming need to be with Alex one more time. Whenever he sees the enemy's face in a dogfight, he knows he is doing this for her. That's all that counts now—even while his life is continually and mercilessly on the edge.

Chapter 29 ∾ Hawaii

Oahu, Hawaii:

A lexa is in Hawaii. While awaiting news about Jack and Midway's outcome, she's following another critical chapter of the war in the southern part of the Mediterranean Sea— the survival of Malta and a possible turning of the tide for the Allies in Europe. Malta is barely holding out. If this tiny island goes down, it will end any hope of stopping the Third Reich in its fanatic march to gobble up the world.

For Alexa, time moves at a terminally slow pace once she knows the Battle of Midway is underway. Jack is in the air, and Leonard feeds her as much information as he can get from an undisclosed place. But no matter how much she has to do to get her stories out on the wire, she's drawn back to Jack, fighting the enemy in the skies over Midway Island, some 1300 miles away from Hawaii.

The two have become one though remaining separated by thousands of miles. She can feel his presence and places all her energy with him. There's no other way to describe it. Like everything else in their affair, she's never experienced this altered state before. Yet the ability to *link* with him comes naturally from a reserve deep within.

It's nearing midnight on June 4th when Leonard finally gets a call through to Alex on a secure line. He has news for her.

Through the carnage of Midway, the Allies have won a decided victory. Jack is alive.

Within hours, there's a dramatic change in the tone and attitude throughout the Hawaiian Islands. After months of only living moment to moment, people seemed to actually breathe again.

A week later, Jack finds Alex in a room lined with radio equipment, typewriters, and large windows open to the sea. Concentrating on something she's reading fresh off the wire, her back is to him when he arrives, now standing at the door. He watches her; she can feel his presence. Turning slowly, eyes glistening, she can't move, wanting to take in the reality of him. They smile together. In a split second, they're in each other's arms. The touch, the feel, the smell of one another ignites their souls once again. On that balmy afternoon in late June, they leave the correspondents' office that overlooks the wind-swept Pacific. They're not seen again for two days.

Chapter 30 ✑ A Lifetime of Memories

A lexa's next assignment would be to go to Malta "if" Churchill and FDR's upcoming plan works. And Jack is to go to the fight in North Africa—in an effort they call *sailors with wings*.

Jack spends the next seven weeks in Hawaii, learning to be a Torpedo Bomber pilot for this critical front. Torpedo bombers planes were used for the first time in the Battle of Midway. And because of their incredible success, the military's training fighter pilots willing to take on this new aircraft, as fast as possible. They need these men desperately in the European theater.

As important as the massive, ongoing struggle to recapture vital territory in the Pacific theater is—the mantra throughout the military and in DC is *"Europe first."* With Midway won it's still wishful thinking that Japan will eventually lose—although there's no doubt that it would be with great cost to both sides. Japan's low on steel and oil—and it's for those resources that she's trying to conquer other nations as fast as she can.

Even with the maniacal tenacity of the Japanese military, the US believes that world peace depends on first conquering the sociopath that is reigning terror across the Atlantic. Many naval flyers are being diverted to stopping Germany in North Africa—thus denying access to the Suez Canal and driving the enemy back into Europe.

Together for seven weeks in the once-paradise that was Hawaii, Jack and Alex try to pack in a lifetime of memories; the only normal life they might ever know.

It's mid-August 1942, and they both receive official orders to be executed immediately. Jack is being sent to the USS Ranger, an aircraft carrier in North Africa, to prepare for the decisive aerial battles that will take place in November.

Alex is told by Leonard that they will be getting her into Malta by any means possible. At this point, all he could say is, "Malta has survived massive bombings for the last three years and is still able to fight the Germans in the sky, cutting the supply lines for their troops in North Africa. You need to promote Malta's importance and the cutting of those supply lines because we're on thin ice in the European theater."

On their final day together in August, they stand on the airfield and Jack's last words to Alex are, "I don't regret a moment of my life, or what I have to face . . . not if it meant that this is how I could find you. Whatever awaits me, you are with me always."

He heads out for North Africa two hours before she leaves for Malta.

Chapter 31 ᕲ A Mediterranean Island

Malta:

M alta is small, highly strategic island in the southern part of the Mediterranean Sea. Before the war this large rock (actually, an archipelago), seemingly in the middle of nowhere, was protected by the British, who had a vitally important naval base on the island. It was abandoned by the British the minute Malta fell behind enemy lines when Mussolini joined the Axis in 1940. And now, with unimaginable sacrifice, it's making worldwide history by repeatedly cutting Rommel's North Africa supply line. For two years, a ragtag group of soldiers and RAF pilots with their wives, along with the brave citizens of Malta, have fought the Germans and Italians while enduring sheer pulverization with more than 15,000 pounds of bombs dropped on them daily. Eventually, Malta will have the reputation of being the most bombed place on Earth.

Even while Malta is being pounded out of existence, in the skies above, the few remaining pilots and planes left on the island earn a saint-like reputation for fending off the Luftwaffe—repeatedly denying German supplies from getting through to North Africa.

Newsreels showing the bravery of Malta in every part of the free world ignite the imagination of people everywhere. The story of this abandoned island offers hope—for which a war-torn world is starving.

After two years of constant fighting, and with the island's occupants only two weeks away from starvation and surrender, a major convoy is launched in the summer of 1942. Churchill and FDR sacrifice critical men, planes, and ships in the convoy that eventually allows the USS Ohio, delivering vital supplies, to limp into Malta's strategic Grand Harbor on August 13, 1942. In the convoy, there were 14 merchant vessels, the most important being SS Ohio—the only large, fast tanker available, and on loan by America to England. It took the Ohio three days to go the last six miles. This convoy was protected by the largest escort force yet: two battleships, three aircraft carriers, seven cruisers, 32 destroyers, and seven submarines. After a long, multi-day, massive air battle over Malta, with every citizen manning guns on the ground, a few precious ships finally get through.

Because of Malta, the tide turns and by fall of 1942, the Allies start the push to drive Germany out of North Africa—retaking Egypt and Libya, allowing Malta to once again became an important base for the British.

Alexa is the first to tell this story to the world.

After the SS Ohio arrived, they get Alexa onto the island via submarine. She has a place to work in Malta's war room—a series of deep underground rooms built originally by the Knights of Templar 500 years earlier. From here, she can stay in constant communication with the OSS, and Malta becomes one of Alex's most important stories. No misinformation, just the truth of what a victory in recapturing Malta means to the Allies—along with capturing the life-or-death struggle behind the island's two-year survival after the British were forced to leave.

Most importantly, Alexa's able to tell the world this story before the German propaganda machine can weave its lies. Public opinion is everything to the war machine.

Chapter 32 ✎ Somewhere Over Casablanca

North Africa, November 1942:

An assembled Allied task force that includes five US aircraft carriers, and four British aircraft carriers . . .

At first, Jack's plane is reported shot down, and missing-in-action. Although Alexa truly believes he is alive, she lives through four days of hell in Malta's dark war room while awaiting word from Leonard. On the fifth day, she's told that the *HMS Avenger*—a Royal Navy escort aircraft carrier—has rescued Jack and several other pilots from the Atlantic Sea.

It's now three months after the USS Ohio made it into Grand Harbor. Several battles have finally secured the island—and Egypt—for the British. Alexa begs to be put aboard the next plane or ship to London. Her request is approved, and in 48 hours, she is on a military aircraft for England.

Chapter 33 ⌒ London's Devastation

London, England:

Alexa arrives in London and is in the OSS office with Leonard. With much difficulty, Leonard begins, "Hours after leaving North Africa for England, the *Avenger* was sunk by a German submarine with a heavy loss of life. It's been confirmed that Jack has gone down with the ship."

Alex nods. But she already knew this—she didn't need physical confirmation.

With this news, her mourning is consuming, like a heavy cloak suffocating her. Alex's unbearable pain is so great that little can get through to her. After several days, Leonard helps direct her through the grotesque fog.

"I prepared you, Alex. Now I need you to be aware of the bigger picture; you can't work on pure emotion. You can handle what lies ahead.

"What lies ahead?"

"That is up to you. But you're either in or you're out."

From then on, only her work brings her out of this nightmare. With Germany on the defense everywhere, London and her citizens are being fire-bombed. Despite this unfathomable atrocity, the world, particularly her enemies, needs to know England is still holding up. She is not going down.

All this comes to pass as Alexa watches the world around her heavily under siege. People are counting their blessings in the middle of devastation and loss—often with nothing physically left. It's the Christmas season—a time Alexa's always loved . . . a time when everything important has great clarity.

From her earliest childhood recollections, she's found a depth of spirituality in the arrival of this time of year. It has little to do with the words she learned to recite in church—although what they taught her set her on the right path.

Alexa's always seen Christmas in the eyes of those around her; even strangers seemed transformed into friends as they passed on the streets. There was something far more magical than festive city lights or the magnificent tree in Rockefeller Center. Something even more than the love she shared with her family on Christmas morning.

For Alexa, it's always been Christmas Eve that represents the immutable promise of what lies ahead—a promise so transformative, one can only celebrate. And now, amongst lost, scorched Earth, and hopelessness, that phenomenon occurs again—with a realization never before imagined.

She knows now that denying the deepest meaning of this ultimate Christmas gift would leave her empty . . . an action far more destructive than the decimated city she sees before her. And the depth of her understanding fills the bottomless hole where soul-numbing pain resided.

On this cold night in London right before Christmas, Alex looks at the stars and thanks God for being given the opportunity to love Jack. She was loved by a man who fulfilled her in a way she knows will never be reversed. Even through the pain of loss, she becomes acutely aware of the meaning of their love and its unending power. This power has no limits . . . a gift to be used in every aspect of her life. Even though the man is no longer here, his love for her will continue to change her.

And then, epiphany strikes: Once changed . . . one can never *not* know that power. She laughs to herself, "Death be damned!"—and is surprised hearing herself say it out loud. With that, she feels his arms wrap securely around her, with his clear, reassuring voice in her ear, "How right you are, my love." She can only smile; she will never lose him again.

In the shambles of London in December 1942, this moment becomes her sacred Christmas gift.

Chapter 34 ∽ The Year Ends . . . The Other Side

New Year's Eve:

The city is again being fire-bombed; it's daily now. Alexa and several others are caught on the top of a building that's burning uncontrollably. It's about to collapse. A strange calm possesses her as she watches wild and irregular exploding stretches of fire erupt across the city of London. She feels the heat, and then she feels nothing.

The Other Side . . .

She's pulled off the top of the burning, crumbling building by a power that's been with her from the day she was born. When the body is no longer necessary, the soul can be helped out before the human shell expires.

He left before she did, but he's been with her every step of the way. She finally hears him . . . feels him . . . sees him before her, allowing her to release the pain of physical separation.

There is no real separation between them. There never has been. Wherever their destinies have taken them—whatever road each soul has chosen—the powerful connection of their love sustains them. Why has it taken her so long to realize that?

Have they both finally learned that it isn't *"being in love"* that makes a difference? It's the *power of love* and knowing how to use it . . . when to use it . . . where to use it. Love has to be earned, felt, and experienced—and it doesn't always fit neatly into the life you are living. No matter how connected, love can be dissipated without proper respect or care. The messenger can be separated from the message.

He knew this, of course, but he's of a different nature. His soul graduates differently. He's been built to attack the world around him at any cost. Not right. Not wrong. Just another set of conditions that he considers to be part of his toolbox.

But for now, for a brief moment, he needs to rest—to understand his growth and see if his actions have made any difference. Only then he'll be ready to decide the next direction.

Different souls, but both are evolving. They're beginning to accept one truth: There are lessons higher than love—but only through the dynamics of love will those lessons be understood.

Each now accepts that ultimately, together or alone, they need to return; again.

SHE: "Are you afraid that I'm drifting away."

HE; "Yes."

SHE: "Then do something about it."

HE: "What—I don't know what to do."

SHE: "Fall in love with me again."

HE: "I don't think that's a choice . . . I *will* find you."

SHE: "Yes. We will meet—someplace new and fresh for us both. I long for a place where sunlight adds warmth and color to our lives. I just don't know where."

HE: "We'll know—we'll be drawn to it. We'll find each other."

LOS ANGELES, CALIFORNIA
⁕ DECEMBER 1996

*There is no such thing as time or space between
two people who love each other.*

That's a good thing . . . but not always comforting
as we become *Earthbound*.

Ah, but life is like a Mobius strip . . . we keep
learning the same lesson at a higher level!

Chapter 35 ∽ Who They've Become

By earth's standards, each destined lover lives a fulfilled and diverse life. Complications, roadblocks, and challenges—taking the form of life choices—never seem difficult to scale. Until they meet.

His life had been planned at an early age, or so he thinks. Raised in an upper-middle-class ranching community in the heart of the Rockies, he always longed for the excitement of the big cities . . . preferably, the world's major capitals.

He was restless from a young age but never really understood what would satisfy him. He attended American University in Washington DC to become a diplomat, a profession that's a perfect match for his talents.

As an adult, his taste have become impeccable, his instincts unique, and his charm easy. Even the most demanding challenges of life, he accepts with a sense of inner knowledge that nothing can stop him from his ultimate goal . . . whatever that maybe.

His only fear: Not living a life well spent.

She was born into a generation that wants to change the world. By the time the full flush of youth was spent, most of her contemporaries were weary and old beyond their years. She sees it coming—her privileged generation's unrelenting rhetoric and unfocused rebellion seemed trite to her. She's determined not to fall into that trap.

For as long as she walks this Earth, she wants every season of her life . . . every year of her life . . . to bring something new. To her, consistently pouring out one's emotional energy in youth always seemed like a defeating way to pace one's life. However, in accomplishing a pace that allows her to fit in absolutely every magnificent thing this life has to offer . . . she knew instinctively would take wisdom and patience. Insight from a deeper resource she's always relied on, well beyond her physical learning—and, frankly, beyond what she actually understands. All she knows with absolute confidence is that she's being guided at any given moment.

Life progresses, and, as an artist, she makes pragmatic compromises. She never regrets the concessions, as difficult as they are to accept. She knows that God's given her something quite extraordinary in the form of three children. Motherhood feels like something quite new to her; she often reflects without really understanding the implication.

She does know from her earliest recollection that she has always had one overriding feeling propelling her through life—an incredible anticipation of what is to come. Something she's here to be a part of as long as she stays on track.

That track—her ultimate life's purpose, is not always clear; but her goals are precise. However, as her life takes form, there are long stretches between major leaps; but she accepts that (some stretches being more manageable than others). There's always something to do while God's lining up the next goal.

Trying to savor everything and knowing that restlessness could be her downfall, she embraces every "normal" aspect of life: babies, friends, entertaining, finances, chores, athletics . . . just living. Nothing is too mundane or too far out of the scope of possibility. Even her lifelong yearnings to sail and ski became treasured family events.

Eventually, she becomes aware that *everything* is part of the plan and that every journey segment requires effort beyond her comfort zone. At an early age, she read a Robert Frost poem—giving her a sense of direction and comfort throughout her life:

> *Two roads diverged in a wood, and I,*
> *I took the less traveled by.*
> *And that has made all the difference.*

Chapter 36 ～ A Friendship Begins

A Journey Continues:

They meet on Earth long after each has woven their life into fabric that is rich, full, and layered. No matter how content and appreciative each seems with their life, there remains an undefinable anticipation only felt in moments of fleeting awareness.

He's a few years her senior, engaging, and smart. But she has a wisdom that serves her well as long as she is uncompromisingly honest with herself.

They know from the day they meet that the other is someone they've already loved. Their laughter is casual and intimate—and their eyes sparkle and connect without embarrassment long after the conversation finishes. In each other's presence, they have the strength to be who they are—only better. Each is nourished by the other in thought and deed, yet, for three years, neither acknowledges the dynamics of their relationship.

They meet at an embassy party in Hancock Park—an old, established, and very wealthy area near downtown Los Angeles. Because of its proximity to the foreign councils' offices, Hancock Park became something of an embassy row during the early part of the last century.

The party is at Christmastime. He is just in from a long assignment in Madrid. In January, he'll be living in Washington DC, as part of the new administration taking office. She's a writer who recently accepted an editorial position with a major magazine specializing in business, politics, and economics.

Heady stuff to some, yet neither seems overly impressed with any of it.

After their initial meeting, where they spent hours talking, their lives continue to crisscross. A couple of times a year, they see each at lavish functions given in one of the major cities across America. These very respectable encounters would be by long dinners and extended phone calls making sure the other arrived home safely. Then, when their high-profile lives take them away from communicating for long periods, a phone call is needed to "catch up."

They discuss everything. Dinners center around politics, arts, traveling, philosophy, sports, and other colleagues—nothing is off the table. But it's the long, easy phone conversations where they discuss life's intricacies, learning everything about one another. They cover every nuance of life: mates, friends, likes, dislikes, childhood memories, parents, children, and even the psychology of living. And always, the dynamics of all conversations are buoyed by laughter.

One day, she finds herself saying a short prayer that the inevitable be put off as long as possible—then moves ahead with life as if the universe will protect her from learning what she's destined to experience with him.

His only prayer, "If there's a chance, let me know when," is quick, to the point, then tucked away for no one to see—allowing him the space to move on with the demanding business of his life.

It happened so easily; neither see it coming.

When their lives finally reach a colliding point—there's no way around it. She feels it's happening too quickly. On the other hand, he easily points out that, after three years, what they're experiencing is rare and to be cherished. Either way, they both know they have a love that has been tested and proven.

It is no longer a man and a woman in love . . . they've become one. Bonded beyond anything they've known in this life. This stark reality came alive with one inevitable, quiet, lingering kiss . . . *A Kiss to Build A Dream On*. It's a dream that they can share with no one. It can go nowhere. It is just, to them . . . *we*.

Chapter 37 ✑ Love's Death by 1000 Cuts

N ow their love runs so hot and consuming it quietly possesses them when they're away from each other. However, neither is a stranger to the demands of life. They're trained to concentrate on that which is before them . . . and, as a relief from being immersed in the depth of their love, are actually happy for life's diversions.

But somewhere, deep in their being, they hear each other. Caught in endless, repetitive meetings, his thoughts turn to her, finding himself silently laughing at some random communication. At night she talks to him in unspoken communication as she moves through the darkened house; checking on whichever visiting college-age child is home. As she continues to her bedroom and, upon seeing her husband's loving face, she puts her other life away.

Neither felt they found each other because of something missing in their life. Both are immensely satisfied with the lives they've built with their mates—loving partnerships and close-knit families that thrive no matter what challenges they face—an increasingly rare and admirable accomplishment.

No. Nothing seemed missing from their lives. But now, something incredible has been added. However, it's because of both devotion and respect for their mates—and for what they've built with them—they know unconditionally that if it comes to a choice, they'll sacrifice each other first.

However, that's not what caused their separation. It was a tear so severe, yet so seemingly unnecessary, it takes agonizing months for her to dislodge from him . . . mentally, physically, and spiritually.

What a shame. And, how inevitable.

The cause? Abandonment. Neglect. A focus so strong on the physical world that complacency seeps in like a silent enemy. Problems—roadblocks to major negotiations—arise for him at work. She understands. She, too, faced challenges. He changes. His "hunters" mode for survival counters any wisdom or logic he may have gained. Again, she understands.

It isn't the silence for days on end. When someone you love is facing a mountain, it takes every resource within them to climb it. Only an insecure clinging vine would demand undo attention.

But this is different. He becomes abrupt, verging on dismissive. Eventually, when they speak, their short conversations end up the same, "I'll catch up with you when I have time."

Eventually, tired of the anger and rudeness directed at her "just because he could," she lashes out.

SHE: Enough! Don't repeatedly shut me down—that hurts.

HE: "I don't care right now—I'm stressed. I can't deal with anything else."

SHE: "So hurting me *is okay*?"

HE: "Damnit, isn't that what love gives us? Forgiving each other no matter what we do?"

SHE: "No. It isn't. That kind of license is granted only to fools. You know better."

The death of a relationship by a thousand cuts.

Sadly, he was enabled throughout his life by those close to him, always giving him some excuse. So, he always struck out where it's easiest when under extreme pressure and facing frustration or fear. And why not? It always felt good—immediate gratification, like a punching bag. It always worked for him. And he was always forgiven or ignored; providing no opportunity for him to think about his actions.

However, now he possesses something stronger with which to face the world . . . and has thrown it away. Along with it, the very soul of their relationship.

Agonizing weeks for her stretches into months. Through the pain, she surrenders. She knows all is lost with him. However, as a sense of peace slowly takes over within her, she understands that she can't give up on what they have discovered together. The messenger's gone; the message remains.

It takes quite a while and much soul searching to understand that it isn't their love that's the gift. Love can come and go swiftly. It's what their love did to her . . . that's the real message. Her forever gift. No one can take that away, and she holds on to that tightly while the pain of bitter separation starts to dissipate.

Three months later, he calls. His voice is warm and cajoling; apparently, his life is on the right track. He has a way about him. Once again, his natural charm is free to weave his magic. There's no doubt he knows what went wrong . . . but is still blind to the consequences.

The long talk starts slowly. Although most of the anger she felt has blown away with the wind of time, the hurt is still raw and heavy within her. She is vulnerable. Still, speaking clearly and without acrimony, she does better than she first expects.

Her last remark . . .

"You absolutely pulverized our relationship. That's on you. But I think I have the strength to move on. For that space, I thank you." She wishes him well, hangs up, and cries for the last time over their incredible love and inevitable, loss.

As time moves on, somewhere in her deep recesses, she knows:

To protect all that we loved . . . something had to be sacrificed. It was *we*.

She almost smiles at the thought—the relief that it no longer has a depth grip on her. Then, she lightly shakes her head with a reflection that refuses to go away:

Yeah, but what a *lousy* way to do it.

Chapter 38 ❧ Coincidence at 30,000 Feet?

Almost three years later:

The early morning flight to New York is full, but she manages to get the last business-class seat. It's late fall—a season she loves, heading to a city she loves. Life is good.

Her new agent is a tenacious, blunt, but caring woman. Renda McQuire is with a top literary agency and has seen something in her most recent work that moves her. As requested, her dynamic agent has lined up high-profile meetings that will only demand a few hours each day. That leaves a large chunk of time to be completely saturated in this ultimate destination. Nothing's as exciting as New York preparing for the Christmas season: pure magic in the air everywhere.

California this fall is windy, with Santa Ana winds stirring up the heat. She reflects on how glad she'll be to actually use the scarf and coat she's carrying as she walks down the ramp to the awaiting plane. Doing her usual secret kiss on two fingers (which she places on the plane as she moves through its door), she smiles at the flight attendant, who happily greets her.

The line stops as those ahead find their seats. Finally, the line moves and, walking slowly through first class, she looks up to see him staring at her. Their eyes meet, and hold. As the breath catches in her throat, she nods slightly and moves on to find her seat in the last row of business class. Two large seats are joined together, and she slips into the seat by the window. It's only after tucking her computer under the seat, she finally feels like she can breathe. At that moment, a lovely older woman sits down beside her.

There's no time to devise a plan of action—or non-action as the case may warrant—for within minutes he's standing in the aisle, smiling. He holds out his first-class ticket to the older woman and asks her if she minds changing seats with him. "We're old friends who haven't seen each other in a long time," is all he says when he nods at the lady's seatmate.

"But of course—I'd love to sit in first class! I've never had that opportunity. Thank you!" With that, the older woman picks up her things and starts forward towards first class—against the flow but happily determined.

As he sits down, he says, "Do you mind? I promise, if you don't want to talk to me, I'll keep quiet for five hours."

She laughs instantly, "Not possible! Of course, it's alright." Suddenly, she realizes how much she needs a drink. With everyone finally settled, she gives the flight attendant her order. Gently connecting her fingers together, she places her hands on her lap—hoping to control the slight shaking.

They chat lightly for quite a while. He's going to meetings at the United Nations, and she tells him what's ahead for her. The weather comes up, as does the general state of the world. He opens up the conversation to what they're both thinking somewhere over Denver. He addresses the elephant in the room.

"I lost everything when I drove you away," he begins. She just looks at him. Turned toward each other in the small space, their knees touch easily. She feels a slight tremor in his legs, and somehow managed to speak.

"Did you have any idea that I was going to be on this plane?"

"None. But when I saw you, I was compelled to find a way to sit next to you. I'm afraid I would have physically removed that lovely old lady if she had denied my request." Their eyes lock, and both laugh gently. Then she looks away, through the small window to the vast sky and clouds beyond.

"Our time is over. We both know that," she says still gazing out the window. Turning back to him, she continues, "But . . . thank you for giving us this time."

The silence remains only for a few seconds. Then he speaks again.

"How's Muriel doing?"

"Mom passed last year . . . quietly. It was hard on both Steve and me."

"I'm sorry to hear. Losing a parent is never easy."

"I don't think it's supposed to be easy. But my brother and I were there for each other. Thankfully, still are."

"She was quite a woman; quite a life."

"Yes, when you start out being rescued as a child on the *Lusitania*, apparently, you're destined for an interesting life. She was one incredible lady."

"Seems you fulfilled her greatest dream for you. You've become the writer she knew you could be."

"Yes . . . with lots of twists and turns along the way. It took me a long time to really love writing. It definitely wasn't the direction I started in, but now I have a true reverence for it."

"It's amazing how dreams have a way of changing, almost imperceptibly."

She laughs softly, "I think it's called growth."

"Mixed with a heavy dose of life," he readily responds with a sly smile.

"Are you still flying?"

"No. It just doesn't hold the passion it once did for me. After I lost you, many things lost their allure. It was as though they were linked with you, even though I'd been a private pilot since college. I never quite understood it."

She looks away again, "I still can't bear the rain."

"Ah . . . being together in the rain was almost like being in church."

She looks back and, for the first time since they boarded, they lock eyes. "Don't."

"I know . . . I won't." He sees the attendant nearby and orders two more drinks.

Chapter 39 ∽ *We* Failed

They spend the next two hours talking about absolutely nothing and everything. Their mates and children and mutual friends they both still see—especially the two people that each has stayed particularly close. Their shared fondness is evident as they discuss them at length: an influential government leader, Leonard Stone, and one of the most successful African Americans in the arts, Charles Jackson.

Their conversation is calm but moves with a rhythm of easy grace. It's as if they're starting over again, only better. They know what questions to ask. They're weaving a friendship. Slowly, carefully, they avoid any intimacy. Yet everything spoken—without any conscious effort—is intimate between the two. Somehow, they know they're giving a grand salute to all that they were.

Somewhere over Kansas, dinner meals are served, giving them both a chance of relaxing together. Silence takes hold without any embarrassment.

It takes a while, but she finally realizes she's ready to open a wound, hoping there might be healing for them both.

"Love is friendship set afire," she says after their trays are cleared, and the attendants are out of earshot.

"What?"

"An old French proverb. First, we had a magnificent friendship—and soon, it was set afire by a passion neither of us could control. But somehow, we forgot the friendship. It was our friendship that sustained the two of us through much. But the love failed us. Or more precisely, *we* failed it."

"*We* stopped existing."

"Yes," she nods.

"On the phone, when you told me that I owned the destruction of *we*, I was confused. Eventually, I realized how right you were. I own the responsibility of destroying our relationship."

"And I stopped trying. I gave up. Maybe it was right based on the lives we had . . . but it wasn't right for us . . . for what we had. We owed it more."

"It took a while for me to understand all of it; what we had and the responsibility of taking care of that gift. Even once you and I came together, I expected my life to move forward as it always had. And, when it was convenient, using the same old excuses to put things on hold. That's the only way I knew how to handle life for a very long time."

"Well, that certainly worked out well," she comments sarcastically. She immediately recognizes her mistake and continues quietly, putting her hand gently on his. "There wasn't much to love, or even like towards the end. And, unfortunately, after a while, I didn't even care. She gently removes her hand from covering his. "I don't understand how others in your life ever accepted your actions. It was brutal. I was hurt in a way I'd never known."

He can't look at her, and gazes pass her out the small window, "I'm so sorry. Please, please forgive me."

"Months later, when you finally called, the man I had loved emerged once again. But I was *terrified* to allow that person back in. I was terrified there was no separation from the man who ran away from life in anger, and the one who returned with unapologetic joy."

Then, briefly, she puts her hand on his knee. With no acrimony in her voice, she continues, "And, sadly . . . with that fear, I found it incredibly easy to give up."

"I had learned to compartmentalize very well," he said, "a trait I learned from my dad . . . or maybe society in general. But I didn't try to stop it—even when it hurt someone. I always counted on cleaning it up later." He puts his gently over hers before she can take her hand away. "Anyway, let's just say I'd definitely been *carefully taught*. However, I'd taken it to the next level by the time we met— I'd perfected it for decades, *all* by myself."

"Interesting," she says carefully. "I don't think it's about what we draw on when times get rough; that's part of our arsenal."

"I'm listening."

"It was about using a power you've gained *beyond* what you already knew. That's something you told me that changed you— through *we*. And yet when you needed it, you rejected that power— and how it could govern your actions in any situation. I couldn't understand it. I tried to tell you that, but I failed repeatedly."

"You're right," he agrees. "I didn't realize I what I possessed. What I found with you was a gift that made me better . . . wherever I turned. I see that now. But using that gift—breaking old habits—would have taken a tremendous amount of effort I obviously wasn't willing to give. Shutting you out was the only way I knew of handling the pressure I was facing."

He carefully plays with her long delicate fingers and then looks at her again. "How sad. And, how simple that sounds. Much later, I understood the dynamics of what I had, only too late."

She nods, "Too late for us . . . for *we*." She turns her hand over and gently grasps his. "But not for you . . . or me."

"I can't see that; all I see is what I wasted."

"Then listen to me carefully, my friend." Her smile is infectious. It takes her a moment to go on. "What I learned . . . what you made me learn . . . was that from the day we met, from the day the power of our love opened our eyes . . . we were responsible to use it, incorporate it into who we were; whether we were together or not."

"Ah, yes. You can't unlearn what you know."

"Exactly. We can blame others until the cows come home. And I tried. But from the day we recognized our love and what it awakened in us, the responsibility was ours, individually."

"We dropped *we*. "

"Right. That very tool—the true understanding and infinite power of love—could have seen us through, whether together or not."

"Well," he smiles again and takes a deep breath, "I am different now. I look before I leap . . . taking in all that's around me." He gives her a quick wink.

"Ahhhh, so *we*—what we gained from being together—is still doing its work! In me too."

He nods in agreement and looks at her beautiful, calm, radiant face. Within seconds, the captain comes on the speaker to announce their landing at JFK airport.

Chapter 40 ～ Acceptance

They casually walk together to the baggage area. The wait is going to be a long one.

Finally, he turns to her, taking her two hands in his.

"Let me know where you're staying. Please."

"No."

"You don't trust me." His laugh is still easy. And she still loves it.

"No. I don't trust *either* of us." She shakes her head slightly, trying to remove old memories. "This is best now."

"Why?"

"I can't be consumed by you again, even though I'm stronger now. In fact, everything in my life is stronger because of you . . . because of what we had." She drops her hands from his and continues, "But we've built our lives apart from each other . . . and that's where we're needed."

"More than we need each other?" He says, almost as a statement, not a question.

"Yes."

He knows she's right. And he hates it.

"What day do you leave?"

"Tuesday afternoon."

"Okay, then let me take you somewhere for breakfast. We'll meet at the little church you love on Wall Street."

"Ah, you remembered." She looks at him for a few brief seconds. "Okay, but it has to be early."

"Great. Breakfast at eight. I know just the spot. We'll meet at 7:30.

Chapter 41 ∽ One Last Time?

It's a cold but bright morning. Heading towards "the little church" (the only name people have used for over a century), she feels an unbridled joy that she's been numb to for a long time.

But that's okay. She once knew that exhilarating joy and lived every second of it fully. When it had come time to let it all go, she had. As time moved forward, she made a habit of not remembering that breathtaking happiness—the very core of what they once had. Now, that, too, is okay.

However, for a brief time, she promises herself, I'll let it back in. I'll cherish it one last time. As she picks up her step in the brisk fall wind, she feels an incredible contentment move through her.

They meet, hug, and smile at each other with a familiar gleam in their eyes. He refuses to let himself be sad. He knows he might never see her again—and somehow, he's beginning to make peace with it.

"I have the perfect place," he says as they walk. "I know how much you love being way up high."

They reach the restaurant, and she looks up. "Oh God, it's beautiful. And I've never been here."

He takes her elbow as they enter the building and cross the massive floor to the bank of elevators. Several early morning executives—men and women with briefcases, all chatting quietly—are with them as they squeeze into an elevator. They're the last ones in, and as the doors slowly close, she turns to him and quietly says, "Thank you. There couldn't be a more perfect spot for us." She squeezes his hand, then lets it go.

Shaking his head with that sly, charming smile, he whispers, "How could I have let the only thing that's ever completed me slip through my grasp?" He winks at her—sharing a sacred warmth as the doors finally shut, carrying them swiftly upwards.

Outside the now-closed elevator, a large sign reads:

September 11th 2001

Good Morning! This elevator is for
WINDOWS ON THE WORLD restaurant.

Welcome to the top of the North Tower.

Have a wonderful meal on the 107th floor
—enjoy the wonder of New York!

Only when you let go—can you finally be together.

Forever and beyond.

* * *